"As a federal judge, I have had to sentence many convicted criminals to significant jail time after they pleaded that they 'got religion.' But Ray Lopez has written a dramatic book about a wanton murderer who really did get religion while serving out a lifetime sentence. As an evangelical minister and former probation officer, Lopez is uniquely qualified to do this, and he portrays the transformation in a beautiful, mystical way that rings of authenticity."

—FREDERIC BLOCK, author of *Race to Judgment: A Novel*

"Ray Lopez's expansive knowledge from being a retired federal probation officer and working as a mitigation specialist gives him a unique perspective and a true voice that's clearly evident in *The Painter*. Serving the past eighteen years of a forty-five year sentence in a U.S. Penitentiary has given me an ability to recognize the detailed reality of his storytelling prowess. Gripping, humorous, and spiritually inspirational, *The Painter* has perfectly balanced elements of an extraordinary novel."

—EDDIE K. WRIGHT, author of
Voice for the Silent Fathers: A Memoir

"Ray Lopez uses his years of experience as a probation officer to expose the evil culture of the criminal world, specifically of La Cosa Nostra. Lopez exposes the pretense of the good guys who fight evil by 'cheating fair.' The criminal's deficient views of God as harsh and ready to punish influence the inner prison walls of their minds. Ray masterfully shows the only way to freedom."

—VINCENT CARBONE, author of
Distracted Driving . . . Crosses the Line

The Painter

The Painter

A Novella Based on True Stories

Ray Lopez

RESOURCE *Publications* · Eugene, Oregon

THE PAINTER
A Novella Based on True Stories

Resource Publications
An Imprint of Wipf and Stock Publishers
199 W. 8th Ave., Suite 3
Eugene, OR 97401

www.wipfandstock.com

PAPERBACK ISBN: 978-1-6667-3691-5
HARDCOVER ISBN: 978-1-6667-9578-3
EBOOK ISBN: 978-1-6667-9579-0

03/08/23

Chapter 1

It was a typical hot, humid June day in the Tri-state area. Gio was in a perfect position to take the shot. The air conditioner was blowing at full force. Carmine Balducci, aka "The Fork," was leaning back comfortably in the front passenger seat. He was an underboss in the Patriarca Family and a well-known killer, suspected of having at least a dozen bodies on him, including the murder of Vinny Carbone, who he killed by repeatedly pounding a kitchen fork into Carbone's neck. The problem was, half of the killings weren't authorized, and it was very bad for business.

Carmine had gone on all morning about all the electronic features in his new Lincoln Continental, dark black with red leather seats. He used the lever on the side of the seat to lean back as far as he could go. Then he went back and forth a few times to the low hum of the electric motor, explaining that the battery had to be on to use all the gadgets. He settled in the lowest position.

They were listening to Sinatra on the radio. They all got a kick out of Frank singing "New York, New York," as they were getting ready to drive to The City for a meeting with Francis Garafolo aka, "The Genius." He was another underboss in the Family, based in Hartford, with a taste for the fancy life, including an apartment on the west side of Manhattan. Balducci was looking forward to explaining to Garafolo why his crew was no longer entitled to a 10%

interest in truck routes that ran from Jersey, through Providence on the way to The Cape.

As planned, Lenny, "The Driver," had pulled into a rest stop on the Hutchinson Parkway in Westchester County to fuel up. Lenny was always the driver on the big jobs and was always ready to provide backup, or cleanup if things got messy. He also specialized in disposal services and had placed several packages over the years in locations known only to himself. Unfortunately, he would slip up on this job, and The Fork's body would later be found in the Connecticut River in Hartford.

He reminded people of Bruno Sammartino, the professional wrestler. The younger guys said he looked like "The Rock." Lenny was 5'7" tall and 220 pounds of mostly muscle, barrel chested, huge arms, and tree trunk legs with a light coating of dark hair over his chest and upper back. He was always on call. He spent his mornings lifting in a local gym and his afternoons at the range, practicing shooting his Glocks with both hands.

He knew to take his time until Gio signaled for him to get back in the car.

The Fork was comfortable. His head was close enough that Gio could see the flakes of dandruff that were always snowing onto Carmine's shoulders. He had notoriously bad hygiene habits, but nobody had the balls to say anything to him about it. He was essentially a fat slob, 5'6" and 250 pounds of sweaty, stinking greaseball. He was mostly bald with a bad combover of oily black hair (thanks to For Men Only) that kept sprouting from the back of his skull. He was crazy and a huge liability.

On the way down I-95 from Providence, Gio had taken out his .22 snub-nose revolver and had already screwed the silencer in place as they listened to Frank on the radio. Frank was singing, "If I can make it there, I'll make it anywhere . . ." and The Fork started laughing.

"Ha-ha-ha, yeah, but that fat faggot genius won't be making that ten percent anymore."

And as Gio began to position his pistol near the base of Carmine's neck, the sun broke free from behind the low-lying clouds.

The warmth of its rays spread across his right cheek, and he saw himself as a 5-year-old boy in the vineyards in Sicily, feeling the warmth of the sun on his neck. He thought about how people supposedly see their lives pass before their eyes before they die and wondered if the same thing applied to those about to kill someone; then the soft recoil of the pistol and the muffled sound of the round focused his attention to Carmine's head which fell forward after absorbing the shot. Gio saw the small bullet hole in the center just below the ears and gently pulled The Fork's body back, so that he looked like he was sleeping. There was very little blood, just like the old guys had told him. They also told him that if he placed his other hand on the side of the head you could feel the impact of the bullet spinning around inside the skull. They knew it was his first kill, and he thought they were just playing with him. The truth—he was scared to death. He was afraid of going to hell.

Two years later, the federal courtroom was packed that fall morning in Providence, Rhode Island. Looking out from the bench, the right gallery, behind the Government's table, was filled with members of local, state, and federal law enforcement. The left gallery, behind the defense, was filled with Giordano Bruno's family and friends. Everyone called him Gio, or Valentino, as the old guys would say, because he looked like the famous Italian silent film actor. It's been three months since the jury returned a guilty verdict of Murder in Aid of Racketeering against Gio for killing Balducci. The murder occurred on June 18, 1988. The Jury had learned that reputed Patriarca boss, Nicholas L. Bianco, and seven associates signaled the death knell of the Providence-based organization, which allegedly had controlled rackets in Rhode Island, Massachusetts, and Connecticut since the 1940s. They learned that Gio was originally from Sicily, having moved to Providence with his parents when he was 6, and he was gaining power and respect within the family. Getting the green light on this hit was seen as a gift, a huge step forward in his career toward becoming made. Several members of the family had been charged in the murder conspiracy and when the guilty verdicts were returned, they all sat stoic except for Gio, who buried his face in his hands.

Senior U.S. District Judge Nunez, a former U.S. attorney, was a judge's judge, a no-nonsense jurist. After going through the exercise of determining the advisory sentencing guidelines, which called for a term of life imprisonment without parole, Judge Nunez asked Gio if he wished to speak before the sentence was imposed. And then it happened.

Gio and his attorney, JR McCormack, stood up, and Gio spoke.

"Your Honor, I want to start by apologizing to the Court, the Government, the jury, and my family and friends. And I admit here today before God and this Court that I did murder Carmine Balducci."

In the time it took Gio to pause and take a breath, there was a collective gasp in the courtroom. The sound of 150 people simultaneously drawing in all that oxygen was the loudest thing heard throughout the trial, like an enormous vacuum cleaner being turned on then immediately shut off. Beyond being surprised, Judge Nunez could almost feel the hair on the back of his neck being pulled toward the gallery. JR quickly interrupted.

"Your Honor, may I have a moment to speak with my client?"

He urgently started whispering something into Gio's ear, while Gio's family and friends were looking at each other in shock, shaking their heads in disbelief and quietly whispering amongst themselves, like a hive of awakening bees. And the buzzing courtroom stopped still when Gio gently stepped away from his attorney and added,

"I also wish to admit, Your Honor, that I was a capo in the Patriarca Family." And the Gallery burst forth with loud cries of disbelief.

"No! What? You've got to be kidding me!"

Gio's wife, Maria, just sat there in the front row. Unblinking eyes stared into emptiness, mouth open slightly, not moving a muscle until she started to gently shake her head, side to side. The news reporters were writing furiously in their notepads, as they knew that this was the first time in an American courtroom that anyone had openly admitted the existence of *La Cosa Nostra*.

Gio doesn't remember a lot about Sicily, but the memories he does have are vivid. He learned about his father's occupation while growing up in Providence. He knew his papa was a regional manager of several trash haulers in New England, and he ran his own import/export business which required a lot of travel to Sicily. It was a great money-laundering operation. Gio's father was also a *capo*. Gio inherited his father's business. His papa was hardly ever home, but Gio was very close to his mama. He was an only child and went to daily mass with her before going to school. And one thing he learned was that it was a mortal sin if you murdered someone. You were going to hell. Not even purgatory could get you off. If his papa had wacked anybody, Gio didn't know about it. His papa was known as the smartest guy on the crew, and Gio figured he was like Pontius Pilate, who didn't kill Christ. The blood was on the hands of the Jews and the hit men. But when Gio was given the honor of taking out The Fork, he knew it was a test. He knew his only choices were kill or be killed, and he figured either way, he was going to Hell. That's why he confessed, hoping there was a chance he could be saved.

Gio's wife knew the company had to pay tribute to the family. It was part of doing business. But she didn't know the real story. No one in Gio's immediate family knew the real story.

The judge took a recess in chambers before imposing sentence. The courtroom was still stirring with tension as the sentence was awaited. Gio and his lawyer sat still in a dead stare-down with the bench. After thirty minutes, Judge Nunez entered the courtroom, and the clerk called all to rise. Everyone, except for Gio and his lawyer, sat after the judge took his seat. Judge Nunez began.

"Mr. Bruno. The Guidelines are clear. A defendant who puts the Government to its burden of proof by pleading not guilty and going to trial—and only after being found guilty admits guilt and expresses remorse—has not demonstrated acceptance of responsibility. That is exactly what you have done. Nonetheless, in your statement to the Court today, you have done something extraordinary and historically significant in the context of our judicial system, as I have been so advised by my law clerk. Without a reduction for acceptance, you are facing a guideline sentence of life imprisonment without parole. This is a defining technical point. Were the court to grant you a reduction for acceptance, you would be looking at a sentence of 30 years to life. The Guidelines have only been around for a short period of time, and as I see it, they are a work in progress subject to rigorous testing and review. Ultimately, I am still guided by the statute under Title 18 United States Code Section 3553(a), which requires me to impose a sentence that is sufficient but not greater than necessary to comply with the purposes of sentencing, those being punishment, deterrence, victim impact, the seriousness of the offense, risk of harm to the community, your own treatment needs, and my consideration of the Sentencing Guidelines. I have considered all these things and impose a sentence of 33 years' imprisonment to be followed by a term of 5 years' supervised release. The court stands in recess."

Gio turned in his chair to face his family as the U.S. Marshals approached him. His wife was holding her head down. She couldn't look at him. Many others sat stunned, shaking their heads. Some were crying. His 18-year-old son, Giovani Jr., was looking at his father with an expression of fear and anger. As the marshals asked Gio to place his hands behind his back and handcuffed him, he saw his attorney talking with the U.S. Attorney, Paul Danbury. Before Gio was taken from the courtroom, McCormack approached the marshals and asked if could speak with his client for a moment. They agreed and stepped back a few feet. McCormack leaned in and whispered into Gio's ear.

"The Government is still willing to work with you if you have a change of heart. They can bring you back for a resentencing under Rule 35 and ask for a lower sentence."

Gio said nothing, looked at McCormack and walked out of the courtroom with the marshals.

Chapter 2

EVERYONE LEFT THE COURTROOM except for FBI Special Agent John Taurino. He was the lead agent in the Patriarca case and was known as "The Silver Fox" because of the premature color of his hair. He went completely gray five years ago, at the age of 30. Investigating the Mafia was his life. There was nothing else for him. It went blood deep. His family was also from Sicily. His paternal grandparents had immigrated to New York City in the 1930s. His grandfather was a tailor and set up a small shop in Little Italy. But when he refused to pay protection money to The Black Hand, they blew up the shop with dynamite and threatened to kidnap their oldest son, agent Taurino's father. John hated the stereotype of Italians, especially those with roots in Sicily. If you were Italian, you were either associated or had an uncle in the mob. It was just another cultural joke, but not for Agent Taurino. After working for the NYPD for five years, he was hired by the FBI and assigned to the Organized Crime Unit. He was focused and empowered. He was on a mission which left no time for anything else—no wife, no kids, not even a girlfriend. The only distraction he allowed himself was powerlifting. He had been a state champion wrestler in high school and had a decent record at Boston College. Powerlifting kept him focused and competitive. It was his meditation, just him and the weights. He either made the lift or failed. John was 6' tall with a very muscular 200-pound frame. He was also a good-looking man with olive skin, which tanned deep brown during the summer. He had a strong dimpled chin, was always clean shaven and had brown, penetrating eyes. His hero was Joseph Petrocino, one of the first Italians hired during the early 20th century by The Irish Army, also known as The New York Police Department. Petrocino was smart and was quickly promoted to detective to lead an all-Italian unit to dismantle The Black Hand. This involved dangerous undercover work. The Black Hand gave birth to the modern-day Mafia.

John sat at the prosecution's table, where he spent the entire trial. He heard the courtroom door open but didn't turn around. Paul Danbury walked across the room, entered the well and sat down next to his lead agent. Paul took in a deep breath, exhaled, locked onto John's eyes, and asked,

"So. what do you want to do now?"

"What do you mean?"

"What do you mean what do I mean?"

"Come on Paul, what are you talking about?"

"You know Gio's the only one who can help us bring down the entire organization?"

"Yeah. And he's not interested. Who knows what's gotten into his head? He suddenly found God, or a conscience?"

"So, here's some food for thought. You know that Cavateo kid is doing time at Big Sandy for armed robbery . . ."

"Yeah? Where the hell is Big Sandy? And he's just a soldier. He can't give us anything."

"It's not what you know that's important but what you don't know."

John got pissed off.

"What the fuck, Paul! Just get to the fucking mysterious point!"

"Okay. So Cavateo doesn't know that we're about to indict him on that VICAR Murder. In fact, so far, you're the only one who has listened to the tape, on which that idiot is drawing us a map. You know he's got Sicilian ancestry, so I guess he got to skip wise guy school . . ."

"Okay, and . . ." queried John.

"And the victim in that case is another Italian piece-of-shit mobster."

Paul knew this description would either set John off or lock him in, and he went for it without giving John any time to respond. "The warden of Big Sandy and I have an understanding. I also have some friends in the designation unit. We could have Gio sent to Big Sandy. No problem."

Paul paused. He could see that he now had John's full attention.

"Yeah. Go on. I'm listening."

"We inform Cavateo of the evidence we have on his involvement in the murder and advise him of a way out from under it that will assure he avoids a mandatory life sentence and earns him huge credit with the family at the same time."

John was now out of patience.

"For Christ's sake Paul, just spell it out!"

"We know the family will be upset with Gio for the dramatic spilling of his guts in court today, and even though he hasn't given anybody up—yet—the higher-ups are going to be righteously pissed off about this embarrassment to the family, especially in the eyes of the other families. Here's the deal we offer Cavateo: To defend the honor of the family, he cuts Gio with a shank, enough to leave a scar, as payment for his bad conduct in Court. And even though it's not authorized, the Patriarcas will never put a contract on Cavateo because his father was made, and besides, everyone knows that he's retarded, intellectually disabled to be politically correct."

"Then what?"

"Then Gio spends time in the Security Housing Unit for his own protection. We tell him there's a contract out on him, and the clumsy kid was the only option at the time; he stays in solitary indefinitely which gives him plenty of time to change his mind."

John was speechless. Paul watched him carefully. Paul knew what he had just done. He started planning after the trial ended. He knew he had raised more than a few eyebrows when he, the U.S. Attorney, decided to personally prosecute the case. He believed that taking down the Patriarcas would be the cornerstone

The Painter

of his platform to get "tougher than ever on crime." His promise
to clean up Providence for good would pave his road to becoming
mayor. He also knew that honesty, integrity, loyalty—all the cliches
of The Bureau—were part of John's DNA. But he also knew that
John was singularly focused on one thing . . . bringing down La
Cosa Nostra. Paul was driven and saw no other option. He knew
he was destined for the governor's mansion and taking down the
Patriarcas would most certainly assure his victory. John wasn't
talking, which was fine.

"Don't say anything. Just take a breath and take some time
to think about it. I call it cheating fair, and I learned it from the
family. That's how they do business."

John left the courthouse and drove home to his apartment in
Central Falls, 10 miles north of Providence up the 95. His third-
floor apartment was in a remodeled tool and dye factory from the
'30s with a view of the Wyatt Detention Facility, which had a contract with the Federal Bureau of Prisons and housed pretrial de-
tainees. It was where Gio had spent the last 18 months. This view
helped Agent Taurino to stay focused on his mission. He thought,
*Cheating fair. What kind of bullshit rhetoric is that? Is that where
we've come to, using the same methods as the enemy?*

Chapter 3

It took six weeks before Gio was designated to Big Sandy. When he asked his counselor why he was being sent to a pen in Kentucky, he was told it was just a matter of bed-space availability. He knew that was bullshit. The Government was one big family, no different than the Patriarcas or the Gambinos, and they were punishing him for not playing ball. He had studied the Bureau of Prisons policy manual given to sentenced inmates and knew the policy was that inmates were to be designated to a facility as close to family as possible. This made sense because regular visits were an incentive for people to comply with the rules. He was told he could appeal the decision, but he figured there was no point. It would take forever, and he would be transferred anyway. Besides, Maria had already filed for divorce, and he didn't blame her. He had betrayed her and her entire family. And even though he was only trying to protect her, it didn't matter.

He had lied to her; just another sin on a list of many. She and her family were all he had. He was an only child, and his parents had passed away within weeks of each other over a decade ago. His mama was only 52 when she died from a heart attack. It was the stress of the life. As early as he could remember, he could see it in her face each time his Papa left the house. He didn't want Maria to have to live the same way.

He thanked God for his only child, Gio Jr. Junior was smart. His grades had gotten him into Harvard, where he was studying pre-law, and hoping to get into law school at Stanford. But what mattered most to Junior was his involvement with Campus Crusades for Christ. Junior told him that he had given his life to Christ and had forgiven his father, just as Christ had forgiven him when he died on the cross for his sins. Gio was happy for his son and happy that he was still in his life, but he didn't want to hear the gospel, especially from his own son. He knew he had committed a mortal sin and was going to hell.

It was a beautiful fall day when Agent Taurino drove to Providence and pulled into the parking lot of Camille's to have lunch with Paul Danbury. It was the place they always went, where they had discussed numerous cases. The colors were in full bloom. It was his favorite season, and he found it ironic how brilliant the leaves were on the verge of death. But he wasn't a philosopher. He was an FBI agent and had to deal with a prosecutor who had apparently gone over the edge. He didn't know where this was going, but he knew he wasn't going along with Danbury's insane plan to pressure the Cavateo kid to assault Gio to avoid a murder prosecution. He was determined to bring that case to the grand jury. The victim was another dirtbag, but he wasn't going to lower himself into a pit where he would bargain away a victim's rights for some perceived greater good, which was no guarantee of anything.

Danbury saw John's old Camry when he pulled into the lot in his new BMW. He backed into the spot adjacent to the car. Their vehicles reflected the difference between them. John's car was just transportation. He didn't have the time or desire to buy a new one. All he cared about was working cases to the end, and he would drive his Camry to its end—like he had with every other car he had owned. Danbury bought a new car every couple of years. It was an extension of his ambition, a symbol of his success. He didn't need a practical vehicle. Susan, his wife of 10 years, was a career academic, working on becoming a full professor at Brown, while serving as the dean of the Cognitive Psychology and Psycholinguistics Program. It was heady stuff, but Susan had a way of explaining it in layman's terms. Paul loved talking with her about his cases and learned enough to give him an edge to cut into some of the defendants he prosecuted when he was an assistant. They had talked about kids early in their marriage, but both were on the fast track and the subject had died down to a whisper.

When Paul entered the restaurant, he saw John sitting in the booth at the back near the kitchen. It's where they always sat. He looked pissed . . . which worried Paul. He smiled and threw up a quick wave as John saw him coming in.

John heard the front door open and looked up to see Paul walk in, smile, and wave. He hated that smile. He had seen it too many times. Paul's blonde hair was always cut tight, perfect, and his teeth were too white. John saw him for what he had become, a politician. He still remembered when Paul was a young assistant U.S. attorney. He used to be a straight shooter. Now he was talking about cheating fair?! He hated those words, but he knew there was some truth there. The question in his mind was how to find it.

Paul sat down facing the kitchen. John always sat facing the door. It was the law enforcement seat, with an optimal view of the entrance and exits. Paul would always get a kick out of watching his agents dance around the table vying for the power seat. But as his teams worked together, these things worked themselves out. John always took the power seat.

Their waitress, Camille, approached the booth to take their order. She was a senior in high school and named after her grandmother, who had opened the restaurant 50 years earlier. Camille had that classic Mediterranean look, dark black hair, smooth, and shiny, hanging down to her waist. She had high cheekbones, a perfect nose, and full lips. She was beautiful.

John wasn't hungry and was content with black coffee. Paul ordered the chicken parmesan and started flirting with Camille. John's anger grew as he watched Paul move his eyes the length of Camille's body before she left their booth and focus on her ass as she went to place their order.

"Why are you such an asshole? She's only 17."

"She may be young, but she knows what she's doing. She knows how to get a big tip."

"Whatever. Let me talk before you get started. First, there's no way I'm going along with your Cavateo plan. Instead, I'm ready to go to the Grand Jury with RICO murder on that punk, and you're going to present the case."

Paul tried to respond, but John raised his hand and continued.

"Let me finish, and when I'm done, I don't want to hear anything from you. I want you to wait and think about it before you respond, just like you asked me to do."

Paul settled back in the booth and nodded at John.

"Go ahead. I'm listening."

"Paul, the only thing you said after the trial that had any semblance of sanity was the idea that a contract hit would be put out on Bruno's life. These are professionals. They're not a street gang. We won't know anything about it, and the harvest of cooperators just dried up. We both know they can get to Bruno inside the BOP. So, when we go to see him at Big Sandy, wherever the hell that is, based on what we know to be the likely truth, we lie to Gio. We tell him that we have evidence that a contract has been put out on his life. And he needs to be placed in the box for his own protection until we can finish our investigation, make arrests, and return an indictment."

John paused then sarcastically added,

"Remember, don't say anything. I want you to take your time and think about it."

He got up and left the restaurant, and Paul's smile was still there when Camille brought him his chicken parm.

Chapter 4

PAUL DANBURY AND AGENT Taurino sat in silence in the back seat of the cab they were sharing on the way to Logan International Airport in Boston, where they were taking a flight to Kentucky. Danbury was studying the organizational chart of the Patriarca Family, placing checks next to the names of the members yet to be indicted. It was Halloween, which Taurino thought was appropriate as Danbury was once again dressed and acting like a prosecutor. The names not checked off were of more interest to him than the others. Those individuals were all connected to the money-laundering operation starting with Floyd Bernstein, long-time general counsel and consigliere to the family, then Mark Anthony (Big Mark) Cantasani, owner of several restaurants and clubs in Providence, Boston, Springfield, and the Cape. He had seen enough. He knew what he was willing to do. It didn't take him long to settle his mind on the plan. It wasn't "cheating fair," as Danbury had offered as some halfcocked rationalization for committing multiple felonies. Instead, it was a lesser harm rooted in truth.

Although they couldn't prove it, they had every reason to believe that if it hadn't already happened, there would be a contract out on Bruno's life. There was still an ongoing investigation, and they were anticipating some strong reaction from the acting bosses after Bruno's sentencing. You could argue that they were protecting Bruno, and the lesser harm of lying to him would be worth the prosecution of the bosses if their plan succeeded. If was the key word.

Taurino tried to quiet his mind and thought about that scene from one of his favorite movies, *Apocalypse Now*. The scene has Martin Sheen's character locked up in a bamboo cage, and Dennis Hopper's character, a lost journalist who had joined Colonel Kirk's devoted worshippers, was trying to explain Kirk's brilliance, quoting Brando's character, "If is the middle word in life." Taurino had a heart for vets. His father had served in the Marines in Korea. He was thinking about an article he read about Hopper taking LSD throughout the filming, when Danbury finished making notes in his file, closed it with more vigor than necessary, held up his pen and said,

"This is this!"

Taurino had heard Danbury use this phrase on several occasions, and it was really starting to piss him off. He looked at Danbury.

"'This is this.' What the fuck does that mean? Is it your version of 'it is what it is,' but with your bullshit spin on it because you're different?"

Danbury turned toward his lead agent, and with a feigned look of surprise on his face replied,

"I'm glad you asked, and it means the opposite of 'it is what it is.' Don't tell me you haven't seen Deer Hunter?"

Danbury knew John hadn't seen it. He boycotted DeNiro films because of his roles as a mafioso. It was John's own personal crusade against films that exploited the stereotype. Before John had a chance to respond, Danbury continued,

"I'm surprised you haven't seen it, because I know you're a student of Vietnam movies."

"Okay, enlighten me."

"So DeNiro is the leader of a bunch of steel mill workers in a little shit town somewhere in the armpit of Pennsylvania. A few of them are going to 'Nam. They're hunting buddies and are taking one last trip into the mountains before DeNiro and two other guys are deployed. He's the man. He's prepared for anything. At one point they pull to the side of the road to take a piss and they're going through their supplies and such when Stosh, he's the guy that plays Fredo, a weasel of a man, you know who I'm talking about? Oh, that's right, I forgot you've never seen the Godfather movies. Well anyway, Stosh has forgotten his hunting boots and knows that Michael, that's DeNiro's character, always packs an extra pair. He starts asking if he can borrow them and he says no. He keeps asking, and Michael keeps saying no until he loses his temper, grabs his hunting rifle, ejects a round, holds up the bullet in Stosh's face and says, 'This is this!' Stosh has no idea what he's talking about, but the audience does. It means that you have to be prepared. You have to pack an extra pair of boots and enough ammo. You have to clean your rifle. You have to be ready for anything. 'It is what it is' is a resignation, a surrender to your circumstances and inability to do anything about it. You get it? 'This is this.'"

Paul ended his monologue just as they pulled up to the departure terminal at Logan. Agent Taurino shook his head and sighed heavily.

"I think you're giving the audience too much credit."

John let Paul make all the travel arrangements. He planned on sleeping during the entire red-eye. Had he bothered to check his ticket, he would've seen that there were no direct flights to the Tri-State Airport in Huntington, West Virginia, and after two connecting flights, and a total travel time of five-and-a-half hours, they were looking at 100 miles and a two-hour drive to Big Sandy in Pikesville, Kentucky. Once they boarded the plane, John settled into his seat, put on his expensive headphones that would play endless white noise and thought, Pikesville, it's probably like a scene from *The Andy Griffith Show*.

Chapter 5

The Huntington Tri-State Airport in West Virginia borders Ohio and Kentucky. As the plane began its descent, John stirred awake with the popping of his ears. He looked out the window and saw nothing but green, then noticed a single landing strip. Paul elbowed him gently,

"What do you think, Ace?"

John wasn't fully awake and not yet ready to interact with the man he once respected as a prosecutor.

"What do I think about what?"

"The beautiful heartland of America."

"Well, I see a lot of trees and a landing strip. Is there even an airport down there?"

"Of course, there's an airport, but only one terminal. You'll be able to see it as we get closer."

"One terminal! No wonder there are no direct flights from Logan."

"What are you complaining about? At least we got to stay on the plane, and you took a nice snooze there I see. I've been in touch with Warden Robinson. We go way back, you know."

"Oh yeah. I'm not sure I want to hear this story."

"No worries, John. It's all on the up and up. Theo and I met about 20 years ago when we were both starting out. He was a correctional counselor at Wyatt and the liaison with the U.S. Attorney's

Office. He would make the arrangements when we needed to meet with potential cooperators. He was at the University of New Haven working on his master's in criminal justice and would drive two hours each way, three nights a week, from his apartment in Cranston to take night classes. He's originally from Rand, West Virginia, a shithole little town. But he went to the University of West Virginia on an athletic and scholastic scholarship. He played football in high school with Randy Moss!"

John took a deep breath, leaned back in his seat, and looked at Paul.

"Frankly, Scarlet, I don't give a shit. What do you have on Warden Robinson?"

"You don't need to worry about that, John. It's just you and me. We tell one little white lie to Theo and Gio and off he goes to SHU. Plus, it's not really a lie. After Bruno's performance at sentencing, they're going to think he's cooperating, and we know it's going to happen, eventually."

The plane was rapidly descending, and the fasten seat belt sign came on. The flight attendant came down the single aisle collecting cans and wrappers. It was a small jet. She was a young blonde with green eyes and an athletic build. As she passed the seats where Paul and John were sitting, Paul handed her his card.

"Thank you, darlin'. Give me a call when you decide what school you're going to attend."

"Thank you, Mr. Danbury."

"Mr. Danbury was my father. You can call me Paul."

As the attendant moved toward the cabin, Paul leaned into the aisle and stared at her ass, rocking his head to the movement of her cheeks swaying back and forth as she walked.

"For Christ's sake, Paul. She must be what, 21?"

"Samantha is actually 22. She just passed the LSATs and she's applying to law schools."

"Oh, I see, and you're what, going to write her a letter of recommendation? I can't believe you. You never stop. And you're a walking cliché. 'My father is Mr. Danbury.' At least you can come up with some original material."

The plane landed smoothly, and the passengers waited while the ground crew wheeled the huge flight of steps to the main door of the aircraft. Paul stepped out onto the first step, paused, and took a deep breath.

"Can you taste that fresh air, John? Can you smell it? It smells like . . . victory." Paul knew John would get the *Apocalypse Now* reference to the scene where Robert Duvall is standing on the beach. He knew his agent. He knew all his agents. He made a point of studying them. He knew that John's personal protest against what he called "exploitive Mafia movies" had some exceptions. They had some interesting discussions during Task Force lunch meetings. John had defended his position by arguing that unlike DeNiro, Duvall had not made his career on mobster movies and *Apocalypse Now* was a psychological allegory on the war, which was based on Joseph Conrad's 19th-century novel, Heart of Darkness. No one else on the Task Force had heard of Conrad, and they all thought that Taurino was weird. Paul didn't care. Taurino was his best agent.

"It stinks," John said. "It smells like jet fuel."

They walked about 50 yards into the single terminal with their carry-on luggage and went straight to Hertz Rental. Paul had arranged to rent a Nissan Maxima. They were in the car and on the road in less than 20 minutes. Paul drove. He always drove. He leaned back in the driver's seat as he entered the ramp onto US-23 South.

"No worries, we'll be there in an hour."

They drove in silence the first half hour, but for the country music station which was the only thing John could find on the radio. Then John asked again,

"Paul, what do you have on the warden?"

"John, I said you don't need to worry about it. You don't need to know. In fact, it's better if you don't know. I never should've brought it up. I was in a desperate state of mind after the sentencing, but you were the levelheaded one, the voice of reason. You were always the smartest guy in the room."

"I swear to God, Paul! If I hear one more cliché out of your mouth, I'm going to shoot myself! No! I'm going to shoot you! Do you have one original thought in that twisted mind of yours?"

"You know, 'twisted mind' is also trite."

"Shut the fuck up! I'm here, aren't I? I'm with you. We're doing this."

"Alright. I just want to say one last thing. As far as Theo knows, it's a legitimate threat, and we are investigating a murder conspiracy against our man. We just don't have any evidence at this point. But we will."

Both men were done and soon enough, they pulled into the entrance to Big Sandy.

United States Penitentiary Big Sandy sits atop a hill in a lush valley, surrounded by a thick forest. The control tower looms above the facility, a symbol of who's in control. They passed by a satellite minimum security camp as they drove up the road to the penitentiary. Paul found this ironic and thought that the proximity of these facilities served to motivate the inmates to become model citizens. He wondered if there was a view of the camp from inside. He hoped there was time for a tour.

Chapter 6

GETTING INTO BIG SANDY went smoothly. John placed his Luger in the trunk of the rental. The Warden had prepared his staff for the visit. Gio had been there for less than a week, which meant that he was still being processed and had not yet entered General Population. Paul had timed it perfectly, hoping it would be a while before Gio joined the herd. He had briefed Warden Robinson before making the trip, and Theodore welcomed them in the lobby after they passed through security. He was a tall, dark-skinned black man with white hair that amplified his skin tone. John sized him up at around 6'3" and 220 pounds but thought he looked more like a professor than a warden of a federal penitentiary. Maybe it was just the glasses he wore at the end of his nose.

As usual, Paul spoke first, another of his MOs, laying the groundwork for the interaction.

"Teddy! How long has it been, ten years?"

He grabbed Teddy's right hand, covered it with his left, and gave a few firm shakes.

"At least that long counselor. How are you?"

"I'm great and cut out this counselor shit. It's Paul."

John fought the urge to shake his head in dismay as the introduction was made.

"Teddy, this is Agent John Taurino, the head of our Organized Crime Task Force."

"Agent Taurino," Teddy shook John's hand, "it's a pleasure to meet you. I've heard a lot of good things. May I call you John?"

"Thank you, Warden." John always kept things professional. "You can call me anything you like as long as you let me out of here when we're done. What you do with Paul on the other hand is none of my concern."

Once he got over the moment of shock at hearing humor from his agent, Paul offered his fake, but convincing laugh.

"Ha ha ha. An agent with a sense of humor. That's what The Bureau needs more of these days."

The Warden led the men to his office, which was down the hall from the lobby, through a locked door and down another hallway that housed the administrative wing.

"Come in gentlemen, and have a seat."

The office had a huge window with a breathtaking view of the valley surrounding the prison, adorned in the full colors of fall.

"It's beautiful, isn't it? I take time each day to appreciate God's glory and to ask him to bring his light into this dark place."

Paul knew that Teddy was raised Baptist, and scripture rolled off his tongue like it was the most natural way a person could speak. He also knew of Teddy's ambition, his dark side, but that had no bearing on their mission. He had begun calling it their mission in the interest of justice, trying to keep that flame burning in Taurino's heart. Teddy sat behind his desk, which John thought must be cherrywood. And again, Paul started the conversation.

"Let me begin by thanking you for meeting with us and arranging this visit."

"I should be thanking you, Paul. Better it comes from the horse's mouth than from one of my staff. An indefinite stay in the Security Housing Unit is not usually well received. Per policy, inmates are in a single-occupancy cell and are only allowed out five to seven hours a week, depending on staffing. And they usually earn their way in, unlike your man."

John decided this would be a good time to jump in.

"Well in a way, you could say that Bruno earned his way in when he made a public service announcement about the Mafia at his sentencing."

Paul interjected.

"Bruno's very smart. We've got his school records, and you know he has an IQ of 160. It's in the blood, I guess. His father got through the life spotless, and Bruno's kid just got into law school at Stanford! I'm sure he'll understand that we're obligated to keep him safe."

"Well, OK then, let me take you guys down to the processing unit, where you'll visit with Inmate Bruno in an isolated interview room. The two weeks in processing is somewhat like SHU. Inmates have very little interaction with each other. The time is spent doing medical and psychological testing, including observation, of course, before assigning a unit. We also study the presentence report and the file we receive from the Government to see if there are any separation orders that need to be addressed. I think you took care of that when you got the judge to recommend Big Sandy."

Paul had met with Judge Nunez in chambers a few days after the sentencing to advise him of their "investigation" and concerns and requested that he make this recommendation to the Bureau of Prisons directly, rather than on the judgment.

John and Paul had never been inside a federal penitentiary. They would usually have cooperators taken from Wyatt and secretly interviewed them at the FBI field office. As they followed Warden Robinson down an endless hallway, they both felt the sensory deprivation, no windows to the outside. They went through three locked doors, all opened electronically, and walked about a quarter of a mile with no sign of life until they came to the Processing Unit. Paul was reminded of the opening of the *Get Smart* TV show where Don Adams walked down numerous halls and through a bunch of automatic doors before getting to the headquarters of Control. This brought a smile to his face—until they came to the interview room. Bruno was already there waiting for them. He hated Paul but respected John. Both had agreed that John would take the lead.

The room was 10' by 10', with light yellow concrete walls and a gray concrete floor. It was lit by a four-foot halogen light fixture. Gio sat behind a small table facing the door, wearing a yellow jumpsuit. There were two chairs opposite him, a fourth chair in the far-right corner and a surveillance camera just above the door. Paul entered first, and Gio's eyes locked on him immediately. He showed no emotion. As Paul approached the table he thought, What's with the yellow? John quickly stepped around Paul's right side and made eye contact with Gio, thinking, Man he looks a lot older than 38. The case had aged Gio considerably, burrowing deep lines in his forehead, pushing back his hairline, and some gray hair around his ears.

They both stepped forward to take their seats, but before sitting down, Paul offered his hand.

"Mr. Bruno, how are you?"

Gio's arms stayed folded on the table, and his eyes remained focused on Paul. They seemed darker than John had remembered. Paul put his hand down, and they both took their seats.

"What the hell is this?" Gio asked.

And before John could respond, Paul said,

"This? This is this."

John couldn't believe what he was hearing and thought, *Paul has totally lost it. Does he think this is a movie?* Gio snapped back.

"What the hell does that mean?"

John quickly jumped in.

"It doesn't mean anything, Gio. We just took a five-and-a-half-hour flight, with two layovers and a two-hour drive to get here. The U.S. Attorney drove, and I think he's just tired and watched too many movies during the flight."

John was royally pissed. They had agreed that he would take the lead. He knew that Paul was just fucking with Gio's mind, which made absolutely no sense. Paul just loved to mess with people, using his power for leverage.

"Let me get right to the point, Gio. Our investigation has revealed that there is a contract hit on your life. I'm sure that doesn't surprise you," John said.

Gio looked straight at Paul.

"Nothing surprises me."

Paul couldn't keep quiet.

"This information is what led to your designation to Big Sandy, but this doesn't mean you're untouchable . . ."

John seized the moment to regain control at this critical point.

"Which is why you're being placed in the Security Housing Unit, the SHU."

"Let's cut the crap and call it what it is, Agent Taurino. You're putting me in solitary confinement!" Gio said, with an edge in his voice like a serrated knife cutting through meat. "What about my wife, my ex-wife, and my son?"

"We have no evidence that they are at risk," Taurino answered. "We've been in contact with them and have offered our assistance."

The knot in John's gut tightened when Paul added,

"You know Gio, may I call you Gio? The Government is still very interested in working with you, and if you were to sign a co-operation agreement, your wife and son could be placed in the security witness program."

John tried to regain control.

"Gio, this is old school. They don't want your family; they want you to die in prison."

Paul jumped back in.

"Gio," (Bruno's eyes were now burning a hole through the back of Paul's head) "I mean Mr. Bruno. This is no longer your father's La Cosa Nostra. Silence is no longer necessary. We have a member of one of the New York families working with us right now."

The room was suddenly filled with that ear-splitting silence. Gio looked at John, then back at Paul. As he stared at the U.S. Attorney, John thought Gio's eyes had just turned a little darker. Gio then ended the meeting.

"Go fuck yourself, counselor."

As the U.S. Attorney and Agent Taurino began the long walk out, the only sound to be heard was the echo of their footsteps down the empty halls and a slight jingle of their escort's keys. Paul broke the silence.

"Well, I thought that went pretty well."

"Go fuck yourself, counselor," John said, as he increased his pace to stay several steps ahead of the U.S. Attorney.

Chapter 7

GIO MOVED INTO HIS 8'-by-10' cell in the SHU during the winter of 1990. There was a metal-framed single bed bolted to the floor with a thin mattress, mattress cover, pillow, pillowcase, and sheet. The walls were 12' high with a single light bulb in the middle of the ceiling that remained on 24 hours a day. The brightness dimmed by 75% at night. At the end of his cell was a small toilet and sink with a quarter roll of toilet paper. That was the allotted amount, so that inmates couldn't clog up the toilets, as some were known to do. There was no window. The door was made of double-thick reinforced steel with a rectangular slot in the middle, large enough to slip a paper plate of food through, and for Gio to extend his hands, backwards, to be handcuffed for a movement. Gio had heard that some inmates threw their feces at the COs through the opening in the door. They would save up a stash to decorate their walls and toss at the guards, who would eventually have to do an extraction so the cell could be cleaned. A team of COs in riot gear would storm the cell to wrestle a naked inmate covered in his own shit.

Gio was allowed out of his cell for one hour a day to be spent in a small, closed-in exercise area about the same size as his cell. He was given this time to exercise and take care of his hygiene. It rotated during the day because only one inmate could be out at a time, always escorted by two COs. A CO would check his cell every hour, which would wake him from what little, restless sleep he received, which was slowly diminishing day by day. There was no clock in his cell, and inmates were not allowed to have watches in the SHU.

Gio started losing sleep after his arrest almost two years ago. His insomnia worsened in the SHU. He started doing push-ups and sit-ups on the hour. The first few months he gained strength, working on increasing the number of consecutive push-ups and sit-ups he could do, and increasing the total number per day—eventually doing 50 and 200, respectively. But at six months, things took a reversal.

Gio was losing his appetite and his strength. His sleep patterns had been reduced to short naps interrupted by night terrors several times a night. He was wasting away, but he refused to take any medication to help him sleep. He didn't trust the Government, which included the Federal Bureau of Prisons and Warden Robinson. They were part of the same family as Danbury under the Department of Justice. He also began having recurring nightmares. The one featured most prominently involved a Catechism lesson with Father Leone. They were memorizing The Ten Commandments. Father Leone was an imposing character, ancient and disfigured with a crooked neck and a humpback. He had a sharp, pointy nose with deep-set eyes hiding behind his thick, white eyebrows, and lines crisscrossing his face under a grizzly mop of white hair.

"Thou shall not kill," Father Leone said. "Murder is a mortal sin which leads to damnation!" he added for emphasis. Father Leone never mentioned the saving grace of Christ, consequently, leaving a clawed imprint on Gio's psyche that he couldn't escape.

He no longer had the strength for push-ups, so he began walking in his cell along the walls and in front of his bed, sink and toilet, counting his steps along the way.

This is how he learned that his cell was shrinking. He didn't know how they were doing it, but there was no question in his mind that it was closing in on him an inch at a time. He eventually started counting fewer steps, and at night he could hear the soft grinding in the walls as they sank into themselves.

Gio also heard demons in the walls whispering amongst themselves in small gnome-like voices, speaking in a mysterious language. He knew that these were the demons assigned to take him to hell. They were coming closer and closer. He could hear their claws scraping the walls, trying to grab him. At times, they would pin him down and try to suffocate him. He wouldn't be able to move or speak, and each time he thought he was going to hell, they would release him. But they were getting closer to the time they wouldn't let him go. He knew it. They were torturing him, and he wanted it to end. And all the while his cell kept shrinking.

When the thought entered his mind, Gio could see the bullet he fired enter the back of his victim's skull. His moment of triumph over evil had arrived. He would steal the taste of his death from the devil's mouth by killing himself. He believed this would earn him a higher ranking in hell and frustrate his demons.

In preparation for his death, he had crawled under his bed to study the bed frame. When the COs questioned him about his purpose and mental health, he convinced them it was just so he could get out from under the glare of the bulb.

He was able to slip his feet through the support bar across the foot of his bed and realized that he could use his pillowcase to tie around his neck and the support bar at the head of the bed. He knew it would be hard and that he would have to be in a weakened physical state. He started flushing most of his food down the toilet so it would look like he was still eating. The demon attacks increased, always in the same pattern: the voices, the scratching, being pinned down by their claws. He knew he had to act soon before he lost his mind and they killed him.

His cell had shrunk down to the point where there was only a small space for him to move. It was time for him to go. He was nearing his one-year anniversary in the SHU when he laid down on his bed for the last time. He was singularly focused on this one thing.

But he was exhausted and began to fall asleep. In that place in between the world and dreams, he heard his mother's voice.

"Giordaaano!" That warm, soft voice, with that melodic Italian accent. She would hold out the 'aaa,' and fall gently into 'no.'

When he heard it a second time, "Giordaaano," he opened his eyes and thought he smelled the scent of lemon his mother loved.

He focused on the foot of his bed, and through the dimmed light, he saw her shadow. He saw his mama, her hair pulled tight into a loose bun, the shape of her body, her apron framing her large breasts and wide hips. Gio was now fully awake.

He sat up in bed and smelled the lemon, the olive oil, the sugar he so loved from all the time he spent with her in the kitchen. He blinked, shook his head, and blinked again, several times. He started to cry. As she spoke his name for the third time, "Giordaaano," she began to project her own light, a soft golden aura, that seemed to pulse along with his rapidly beating heart.

"No, Giordaaano, no, it is not so, it is not so . . ."

He tried to move but was unable to do so, nor could he speak. He could only breathe and feel his heart pounding in unison with her pulsing aura. But he fought it, with all his might, all his soul. He wanted to hold her; he wanted to be with his mama. He wanted to call out to her.

Finally, as if it were his last word, he whispered, "Mama." And she reached toward him, with outstretched arms.

"No, it is not so . . . Romani dieci, nove . . . Romani dieci, nove . . . Romani dieci, nove."

The light bulb began to flicker, further illuminating her. Then it sparked and burned out, shattering into small pieces falling to the floor.

Gio sat in total darkness and thought, *Romans 10: 9 . . . what is that? Mama, what is this, Romans?* He was exhausted, fell back on his bed and continued to cry and smell lemon until he fell asleep.

Chapter 8

DURING THE YEAR GIO spent in the SHU, a lot of things had changed in the world. There was now a Republican in the White House, and most of the Democratic U.S. Attorneys had been replaced. Paul Danbury left the U.S. Attorney's Office and was now focused on his campaign. Warden Robinson took an early retirement, and the new warden was reviewing all the cases in the SHU. These are the things that came to be by the time Gio rose on the morning after he saw his Mama's ghost. He hadn't slept so soundly in years.

The sound of the CO's key, opening the lock on the cell door, echoed down the silent hallway of the SHU. It was 6 a.m., and most of the inmates were still sleeping. The hallway lights were on and illuminated Gio's cell. The two COs noticed pieces of the shattered light bulb on the floor.

"What the hell?"

"It happens. The wiring in this place is ancient."

"Hey buddy, Wake up. You're leaving the SHU today."

Gio didn't stir.

"Gio, wake up—wake up."

Gio was sleeping on his side, with his knees bent toward his chest, like he used to lay as a child. He was dreaming of his childhood in Sicily, running through the vineyards at dusk on a summer day. He heard his father calling, "Gio . . . Gio . . . Gio . . ."

The CO started to gently kick Gio's feet to wake him, like the angel had to kick the Apostle Peter when he led him out of jail. Gio thought he was still dreaming as he sat up in bed. He stood up but was unstable on his feet. He was dehydrated and had lost weight the past few months, dropping from 185 to 150 pounds. The CO gently took Gio by the arm, as the second officer stood behind them. As they left his cell, Gio paused and looked back. He still smelled lemon and olive oil and for a small moment, he saw rays of sun slicing through olive branches.

"Where are we going?" Gio asked.

"Well, first you're going to spend a couple of weeks in the infirmary," answered the first officer who had called out Gio's name.

"And then you're going into general population."

Guys like Gio, made guys in La Cosa Nostra, were typically untouchables, but he had arrived with some notoriety. His statement at his sentencing was a national story. The Department of Justice and Bureau of Prisons had done its due diligence as far as separation orders go, so there wasn't another member of the Patriarca, Bonnano, Gambino, or any of the other families in Big Sandy. However, mobsters were known to contract hits with outside groups on occasion, and there was one recent case that involved a set of the Bloods in the Bronx, who were paid to murder an underboss in the Bonnano family. It was a bloody mess and involved a classic Shakespearean tale. The son paid for the murder of his own father. The Bloods shot him to death at a McDonalds drive through and everybody got indicted.

After his time in the infirmary, when Gio first walked through the open floor area on his unit, he could feel 50 pairs of eyes following him. He sat down at an open table and started reading the copy of the *New York Times* that Gio Jr. had recently sent him. He had only been on the unit for a week. He hadn't been assigned a cellmate yet and had stayed in his cell catching up on letters from his son. He would soon find out that God had scheduled a divine appointment for him.

Alex "Big Ears" Martinez, the former president of the Spanish Disciples in Kansas City, was serving three consecutive life sentences for ordering a drive-by shooting in which three people were murdered, including an innocent seven-year-old boy. The other two victims were members of the South Dale Bloods in Kansas City, suspected of being responsible for a robbery of a stash house operated by the Spanish Disciples. One Disciple was shot to death and a second was left a paraplegic. One of the scouts on the block made the car and a partial plate before it left the scene. Other Disciples knew the car belonged to Brian Brown, who always rolled with his cousin, Ricky Washington. Alex gave the green light. He cautioned his shooters to make sure there was no one else in the car, other than Brown and Washington. Brown's son, BJ, was asleep in the back seat and killed when the car was shot up with multiple 9mm rounds.

The eyes on the floor always followed Alex when he moved through the unit. He was 21 when he arrived and had packed on 40 pounds of muscle in the past fifteen years. Like Gio, he was raised Roman Catholic, but his mother hadn't taken him to daily mass. She spent her days selling her body on the street so she could afford at least one rock of crack a day. Alex was raised by his grandmother, on public assistance, along with seven cousins. He spent his first ten years in the BOP playing the game, essentially the same thing he did on the outs: selling drugs, gambling, running numbers, and when needed, calling the shots, both inside and on the street. But that all changed five years ago.

Alex stood 6' tall and weighed 240 pounds. He lifted weights when he could but built his body with pushups, a thousand a day, in different variations: one handed, forehead triangles, clapping, deficits (with his feet up on his bed or a chair)—plus 500 dips a day. When giving inmates training advice, Alex would explain how the triceps were the larger muscle group, making up the bulk of the size of one's arm. He also did makeshift pull-ups when he had the opportunity.

Alex had ink over 90% of his body, including a Christ head on his right biceps and the Virgin Mary covering his back. The rest were gang and prison tattoos, telling a story of destruction. His last name, Martinez, was tattooed across his throat, connected around the back of his neck by barbed wire. He was dark-skinned and handsome. His face was clean but for the teardrop tattoos charting his years in the system and the three-inch scar across his left cheek. It was the price he paid for leaving the Disciples.

When he arrived in the BOP, his determined severity level and designation was based, in part, on his identification as an active member of what the BOP defined as a Security Risk Group (SRG), like the Spanish Disciples. Being in an SRG limited an inmate's programming opportunities in education and employment. These restrictions were designed to motivate inmates to disavow their membership or association with an SRG, and the BOP offered a program for inmates interested in doing so. Word got out quickly, both in Big Sandy and Kansas City, when Alex completed the SRG Program.

He was an old-school Disciple and was jumped into the gang when he was 15, back in the 70s. This involved having to fight several other gang members at the same time until you were beaten down and could no longer stand. Back then, a Disciple could gradually retire into OG status, typically in one's late 20s or early 30s, when family and raising kids became a priority. Or a Disciple could be jumped out for personal reasons, in the same manner he was jumped in. Through his leadership, after entering prison, Alex had changed the Disciples into more of a community organization. If you were from the neighborhood, you were accepted, but there was no pressure to join. He also started organizing toy drives during Christmas, clothing drives for the homeless, and encouraged members who had left school to pursue their GEDs. He believed in these things and hoped it would reduce the law enforcement presence in Disciple territory. Otherwise, it was business as usual, mostly selling narcotics.

Since Alex was old school, when news of his departure from the gang became known, his replacements decided to give him an old-school send-off to make a statement and leave him with a permanent reminder of where he came from. It was a simple hit.

Two young Disciples had been designated to Big Sandy, one on a robbery conviction and the other on a 10-year mandatory minimum drug case. They were in their early 20s, known as gladi-ators to the old-timers. Alex knew who they were. He knew all the Disciples, but he didn't have eyes in the back of his head. The kid that approached him was talented, and Alex gave him the benefit of the doubt when he started asking him about the SRG Program and the Bible study Alex was leading. When it's done correctly, it always happens quick. He barely felt the shank that ripped through his cheek and watched the back of his assailant's orange jumpsuit as the young man walked away and was bumped into by another inmate, transferring the weapon for quick disposal. The eager young Disciple who had first engaged him simply walked away. There was a lot of blood, and Alex received sixteen staples. He added their names to his prayer list and moved on.

When Alex walked among the others, he stood tall and saw everyone. But it wasn't just his physicality that drew attention. There was something different about him, a light you could see if you looked hard enough. He had given his life to Christ, and God had given him a gift. Everyone called him The Prophet.

Chapter 9

ALEX DIDN'T CONSIDER HIMSELF to be a prophet, but he believed in the powers of the Holy Spirit, and through his Bible study group, he came to understand that prophecy was real. He was a natural evangelist and had led dozens of men to Christ during the past five years. People listened to him for many reasons—his physical presence and reputation among them. When he started carrying his Bible around, men quickly took note. Some thought it was a scam, as inmates were known to go to church and attend Bible studies, not to grow closer to God, but to make nefarious plans of one kind or another. Regardless, Alex always drew an audience. Some men saw him as weak and his newfound faith as a copout. But others saw the light—the aura around him—and were curious. Evangelism came easy to Alex because he was a good storyteller, and his favorite story was how he came to Christ.

His testimony was powerful and how he first heard about prophecy. His grandmother would read him the Bible when he was young and tell him stories of the great prophets like Isaiah and Elijah. But it was Old Testament, as Old School as you could get. Alex didn't know it was still happening until he met Hector Jackson.

Hector was in his late 60s. He was another lifer. There was an unspoken kinship amongst all lifers. Hector's skin was blacker than anyone Alex had ever met, and his full head of white hair almost made him appear as a living photo negative. His face was distinguished by a roadmap of lines that Hector would say told the story of his life. He was short, about 5'6", skinny, and walked with a pronounced limp. Hector had shot and killed a guard during a bank robbery in Biloxi, Mississippi, in 1965. He was ancient. Nobody paid much attention to Hector and pretty much left him alone. But it was God's plan that he become Alex's roommate. Alex knew that Hector was a Bible Thumper. He was always quoting scripture and offering to pray for people. Most just viewed him as a crazy old man. That all changed for Alex when Hector gave him a word of knowledge one early morning when he couldn't sleep.

"God knows, you know," Hector said.

"What are you talking about, old man? Be quiet. I'm trying to get some sleep." "Alright. He knows, that's all. He just wants you to know that he knows and understands."

"Alright, old man. Just be quiet. I need to sleep."

"Ok, Alex. He knows, that's all, and he wants you to know it's alright."

Alex stared at the ceiling, which was always illuminated by the light outside their cell. He thought, *That crazy old man. He's always talking to God out loud as if he was walking beside him, always quoting the Bible.* Alex could hear Hector breathing more heavily and knew he had fallen back asleep. *He knows,* Alex thought . . .

Time crawled slowly in that cell . . . Alex listened to Hector's breathing, his soft snoring, his rhythm, which was occasionally jolted by a snort. Sometimes he heard Hector laughing in his sleep, but not tonight. He was just breathing tonight. Alex tried to concentrate on his own breathing, in through his nose, out through his mouth, deep and controlled. He had learned this technique to clear his mind in a meditation class, but he couldn't clear his mind. He knows . . . God knows . . . He knows.

"Hector. Hector. Hey, old man! Hector, wake up."

Hector was a light sleeper, often switching positions to run from his pain. He turned toward Alex and opened his eyes.

"He knows what? What does God know?" Alex asked.

Hector slowly sat up and placed his feet on the floor. He took a deep breath and looked at Alex.

"He knows that you had hate in your heart for your mother that day when you saw her in the park smoking that rock. He knows and wants you to know that you are forgiven."

Now Alex thought he might be dreaming so he sat up, placed his feet on the floor and looked across the cell at Hector. There was only a few feet between them. Hector had his hands clasped together, fingers interwoven, and was praying softly in his old man voice.

"Lord, thank you for this word you have given me for Alex. May he be blessed by it and healed."

The words drifted away from Alex, and he saw himself in the park, watching his mother curled up on the end of a bench, wearing a brown hoodie with oil stains on the arms. He was 8 years old. He could hear the voices of his tormentors, the older kids from the neighborhood and school. "Crack baby, hey crack baby! Your mother sucks cocks and crack pipes." And he hated her that day in his heart and screamed in his mind, *I hate you! I hate you! I hate you!*

Suddenly, Alex started crying and laughing at the same time, which he had never experienced. He felt out of control. He was proud that he couldn't remember the last time he cried. Even when his abuela died and they wouldn't let him go to the funeral, he didn't cry or get teary-eyed. But he couldn't stop himself. The harder he tried, the more the tears and laughter came. He thought he might be going crazy and was afraid others would hear him.

He couldn't stop himself. His body started shaking. It was almost like he was outside of himself. His sobbing was deep, like a wounded animal, interrupted by a sort of reckless laughing. He didn't know what was happening to him. He tried to catch his breath and leaned forward to rest his chest on his knees. He couldn't see. His eyes were flooded. He started having a hard time breathing, as his nose was filling with snot. He thought that it would never stop, that he would keep crying and laughing until he died.

He felt someone sit down next to him on his bed and felt a skinny arm reach around his shoulder. He thought it might be God for a moment, but he could smell Hector—that old man smell—and rested his head against Hector's chest. He let Hector rock him slightly, back and forth, and could hear Hector's voice, "Thank you,

Jesus. Thank you, Jesus. Thank you, Jesus," as he felt himself being lowered back down on his bed. Alex slept like a baby for the next several hours.

After that, Alex began studying the Bible with Hector in their cell. They took it slowly at first. Hector was a good teacher, and Alex was a fast learner. Hector had been leading a larger Bible study with other inmates for years and attended Christian services twice a week. But Alex wasn't ready to jump into all that, not just yet. He was confused about what had happened to him that morning. But Hector was patient. He told him God would call for him to step out of the boat when the Lord knew the time was right, and Alex was ready.

Alex loved books and had always been an avid reader. His two favorite novels were *Moby Dick* by Herman Melville and *The Adventures of Huckleberry Finn* by Mark Twain. In fact, his love for literature had grown during his time in prison. He was close to earning his bachelor's degree in English and had begun tutoring men to help prepare for the GED. He was fascinated by the Bible, from a historical and literary perspective. The thing he most wanted to learn about was what Hector called the gifts of the Holy Spirit, especially prophecy. How did God speak to us? How did Hector know about his life, the things he kept secret, hidden in his heart, the things that made him strong? He knew what had happened, but as real as it was, it was still like a dream to Alex.

Hector loved Alex and adopted him as the son of his heart for God. As much as God loved Alex, Hector could see that the enemy was still at work in his life. There were expectations of evil, fear and suspicion. But understanding the Bible was a good start, and Hector loved doing daily devotions that Alex devoured with a hunger for increasing knowledge: Who is the writer? Who is he writing to? What is the zeitgeist, the religious, social, and political forces at work? Memorization came easily for Alex, and Hector waited for God to open the next door.

Chapter 10

HECTOR HAD A PROPHETIC gift but was not an eloquent evangelist. But on this day, God gave him the words of a well-worn-out cliché to get things started.

"Alex, you know when they say to someone, 'Put the cart before the horse?'"

"Sure. I see it all the time, especially in Government."

"Well, God wants you to know that's what you're doing with His Word, and that's straight from the horse's mouth."

Hector knew that didn't come out the way he wanted. When he was a young boy, always impatient to learn, his father used to say to him, "Slow down, son. You're putting the cart before the horse." He eventually came to understand what his father was trying to teach him. Learning a thing was one thing, but there was something else more important, a feeling for a thing in your heart, a passion. The other thing he blurted out, he had always heard from his hot-tempered mother, who was full-blooded Choctaw and too proud, as his father used to say. He remembered his mother telling him that Mississippi comes from the Choctaw word meaning "Father of Waters." He remembered how people from town, people who hated them, would talk ill of his family. And when he heard people say things like, "There's nothing nastier than a mongrel half-breed Indian nigger boy," he knew they were talking about him. Some white people would say things like this, just above their breath, loud enough for them to hear as they walked by, his mother squeezing his hand tighter as she increased her stride. And when his father would come home from the fields at the end of the day, and she would be telling him about those nasty white ladies in town, what they had said about their boy, her face would become scary with anger. And she would say to his father, "I'll tell them what they are! I'll tell them—right from the horse's mouth!"

Before God had pressed upon his heart to go all evangelical on Alex, Hector had read the story about Balaam in Numbers in his Bible that morning, and how God spoke to Balaam through the mouth of a donkey, which made him think about his mother. He believed that phrase, from the horse's mouth, came from this story about Balaam. He believed that all those old sayings people use come from the Bible.

And when Hector heard Alex's voice from off in the distance, like deep in the woods but coming closer and closer—"Hey old man. What are you talking about, from the horse's mouth?"—he knew he had gone off to that place where God folds and unfolds time and takes him back. And he was back in their cell where he was facing Alex. He asked the only question he knew to ask.

"Alex, have you ever asked Jesus to come into your heart? Do you know him as your Lord and Savior?"

"What are you talking about, old man? I've always believed what mi abuela taught me. I've always believed in Jesus and that he's forgiven me for all my sins, past, present and future."

"But have you ever asked him, out loud, to be your Lord, to come and dwell in your heart?"

Alex looked at Hector with that deep, familiar, far away stare. "I guess not."

Hector felt God's hand on his heart and surrendered.

"Man, you are so into the Word, and it excites me because it focuses me on what he wants me to hear. In Matthew 22:37 Jesus says, 'Love the Lord with all your heart and with all your soul and with all your mind,' but I think you've reversed the order, brother. You're all mind, heart and soul, the cart before the horse."

Hector could see some focus now in Alex's eyes. He was listening, and God brought Hector to that verse He had written on his heart so many years ago.

"Romans 10:9 says, 'If you declare with your mouth that Jesus is Lord and believe in your heart that God raised him from the dead you will be saved.' It's the word of God, brother. God wants to hear your voice."

And just like that, Hector knew that Alex was ready. The rest was easy.

"Alex, have you ever asked Jesus, out loud with your voice, to come into your heart and be your Lord and Savior?"

And Alex was like that little boy again in the park, so angry, so hurt, so frightened. And as he shook his head side to side, he could feel that wave coming in again, he could hear his own beating heart.

"Do you want to pray with me now and ask Jesus to come into your heart and be your Lord and Savior?"

But Alex couldn't speak. He could only nod his head up and down.

"So, let's pray together. A simple prayer, but the words aren't as important as what's in your heart, Alex. God knows your heart."

And Alex repeated the prayer led by Hector, in a weakened state, almost a whisper, but he spoke it with his mouth.

"Lord, I know I'm a sinner."

"Lord, I know I'm a sinner."

"But I believe that you died for my sins on the cross and rose from the dead."

"But I believe that you died for my sins on the cross and rose from the dead."

"And Lord, right here, right now . . ."

"And Lord, right here, right now . . ."

"The best way I know how . . ."

"The best way I know how . . ."

"I'm asking you to come and live in my heart and be my Lord and Savior."

"I'm asking you to come and live in my heart and be my Lord and Savior."

"Amen, amen, amen," Hector said.

And that wave came in again, crashing through Alex's heart, and for the second time in his life, he found himself laughing and crying at the same time, and he didn't care who heard him. He didn't know yet that God was baptizing him in the Holy Spirit. But he would learn.

Chapter 11

ALEX STARTED HAVING THE dreams about a year after Hector died from prostate cancer, around the same time he took over Hector's Bible-study group. It was always the same. God would shake him awake from the dream, and it was like he had just seen a powerful movie. The images would stay with him. He wouldn't even have to write them down, although sometimes he did when they were complicated or confusing. Most times, another inmate would be in the dream, and Alex would dwell on it until he took some type of action. Some dreams would involve brothers in his Bible-study group, but others concerned men he had never met. Sometimes he would just talk to the guy to see if the conversation led anywhere, but he would always feel that tug in his gut and tightness in his heart if he just left it at that. Hector had told him that feeling was a conviction of the Holy Spirit.

The truth was that Alex was afraid, just like he had been when he first started sharing his faith. Sharing his testimony and relationship with God eventually became natural to him. It was easy. It was just a matter of seeing who God had for him to minister to, rather than making that decision himself. And he came to understand that he wasn't an agent or broker for God. He didn't have to close the deal securing one's salvation, although many men prayed a salvation prayer with him. He just had to be obedient and love others by sharing the Gospel.

But this prophecy thing was totally different. What if men thought he was crazy? What if it wasn't from God but his own dreamlife, his own imagination? The brain was the most mysterious part of the flesh. At times he would just let it go. Other times he would go for it, only to find out that the dream, the word of knowledge, was totally inaccurate and had nothing to do with the man's life. Alex finally came to understand that it was a matter of faith, and his compass was that conviction of the Holy Spirit. He came to understand that you are who God says you are. You can't hide from it. You can't run from it. You can deny it. You can try to ignore it, refuse it, but it will eat away at you until you are true to yourself and in doing so, true to God.

The dream Alex had about Giordano Bruno was the most vivid and detailed of any dream he had so far. There was a young boy sitting with his mother in church, in the front pew, listening to a young priest, speaking in a language that sounded a little like Spanish, but it wasn't Spanish. The boy and his mother went up to the altar, received Communion, then went to the side of the altar, lit three candles, and kneeled to pray. Somehow, Alex knew the boy in his dream was Bruno. He just knew. Unlike his other dreams, this was recurring, and it was always the same dream. Exactly the same.

Gio was also having a recurring dream of going to daily mass with his mother, every morning, at 7:00 am. He held her hand as they walked down the aisle, past the scattered few parishioners. They would genuflect, make the sign of the cross by touching their foreheads, the center of their chests, and across both sides, the Father, the Son, and the Holy Spirit, and sit in the front pew to their left.

Alex's heart was beating through his chest that morning as he crossed the cafeteria toward the table where Gio sat by himself, drinking coffee, and reading the *New York Times*. Alex started doing his breathing exercises, in through the nose, out through the mouth, and his mantra, be still, in through the nose, out through the mouth, be still, in through the nose, out through the mouth, be still.

Gio glanced up from the sports section and saw Alex approaching.

"Good morning, Mr. Bruno."

Gio looked up from his paper, his reading glasses resting on the end of his nose.

"Good morning."

Gio returned his focus to the story he was reading about the Red Sox.

"Do you mind if I sit down?"

Gio raised his eyes toward Alex and this time focused on his eyes and body language. He appeared to be nervous and was breathing deeply. Gio watched Alex take a breath, filling his solar plexus, then out through his mouth. His hands were folded over his lower abdomen with interlocked fingers, a sign of non-aggression.

"Sure. Be my guest."

Alex sat down across the table from Gio, who returned his attention to his paper and thought, *well, this should be interesting.*

Alex took another focusing breath and thought, *there really is only one way I know to do this. God has used it before. Okay, here we go again, Lord.*

"Mr. Bruno, I know you don't know me, and we've never met before, but God has given me a word for you and as crazy as that might sound, I have to share it."

Gio looked up and focused on Alex's eyes. They were clear. Alex's hands were still folded together, but he was holding them at the bottom of his chin. He no longer appeared nervous to Gio; just the opposite, he appeared to be at peace. Gio decided to go for it.

"Okay, what is this word God has for me?"

Alex took another focusing breath.

"He saw you at Mass every day with your mother. He was there with you both, every day."

Gio heard the words Alex spoke, but they sounded like an echo, somehow distant and fading away. He looked at Alex, tilted his head to the right, like he always did when he was trying hard to listen and stared into his eyes. And for a moment, Gio felt like he was lost somewhere between this day and his childhood.

The memory of his dream that morning was still fresh in his mind when he had been approached by this man, and he could see it again now, he could feel the warmth of his mother's hand, he could smell the incense from the burning candles. Then he heard his name being called . . ."Mr. Bruno. Mr. Bruno . . ." His mind came back into focus, and he was still staring at Alex, his head still tilted to the right. And Alex, having delivered the word, was ready to make as graceful a retreat as possible.

"Mr. Bruno, I'm sorry to have bothered you. I'll leave you to your paper. Again, I apologize."

"What did you say your name was again?

"Alex, Alex Martinez. Some people call me Big Ears for obvious reasons."

And after that day, neither Gio nor Alex had that dream again.

Chapter 12

PROPHECY IS POWERFUL, UNDENIABLE, and without any explanation but God. Alex was relieved. In bringing that word to Gio, he had felt like Ananias bringing the Gospel to Saul. The evangelist in him wanted to charge forward and lead another lost soul into the Kingdom, but he knew it was up to God. He knew it was a powerful word, a bullseye from Heaven. He saw it in Gio's eyes. And he also knew that as much as he wanted to talk to this man about the Gospel, he needed to be still and continue to pray without ceasing.

When he first read that verse in 1 Thessalonians 5: 17,18, "Pray without ceasing. In everything give thanks: for this is the will of Christ Jesus concerning you," he couldn't clearly see the application in his own life. He received the gratitude part and could aspire toward that ideal, but how could he pray without ceasing? He had to move through the day. He had his job in the library, was tutoring men, and leading weekly Bible study and prayer meetings. But that is where mindfulness brought him to a place of understanding, that prayer takes many forms, like meditation. Each breath brought him closer to Christ, literally. He would talk to Jesus throughout his day as he navigated through his circumstances and see and hear God's responses in others.

And he had learned about praying in the Spirit, what he first thought was crazy gibberish coming out of Hector's mouth as he was talking to himself. But he had received that gift which was just between him and God, which gave him further freedom to pray, without ceasing.

Since meeting Alex, Gio could think of little else than what he was told. He was no longer having the dream, but the memory was a constant imprint on his mind. He came to believe that God was punishing him, that Big Sandy was purgatory. The dream had been a reminder of God's love and what he had lost when he committed murder. But he was also drawn to Alex. God had clearly spoken through him, and he wanted to get to know this man.

Alex hadn't approached him since that morning, but they had seen each other on the unit and in the yard. There was eye contact and the obligatory head nod of respect.

Gio began to study this man. There was a presence about him. When he walked by, men would look toward him with a sense of expectancy, or they would struggle not to look his way. When he would sit with other inmates, he would talk as much as listen, laugh and then become quite serious and intense, speaking with obvious passion, not only with his mouth but with his eyes and hands as well. He would often touch men with a handshake or a hug, not a ritualistic dance of orchestrated movement as so many inmates were doing, just a simple and straightforward exchange.

Gio found himself thinking about Alex and feeling a strong urge to speak with him, but he wrestled with his own fear. Would God use Alex again to punish him with memories of lost love and images of the punishment that awaited the unforgiven?

Gio had always fought through his fears. If God meant to punish him while he was here at Big Sandy, he deserved it and should present himself to the Lord. If God could speak through Alex Martinez, he wanted to know this man and hear what else God had to say about his life.

Gio started going to the library on a regular basis. Inmates who had reached the level of trustee had access for an hour a day. Gio had been working as a trustee on food carts for several months. It was perfect for him, as he had very little interaction with other inmates. His job was just to bring the carts to the units and return them to the kitchen once meal service was complete.

Alex saw Gio right away when he walked into the library. They saw each other and exchanged head nods. Alex was reshelving books in the law section. Most inmates spent time in the library on the computers and reading law books to research possible appeals on their cases. Gio had decided to read the Bible.

He had never even opened a Bible before. There was one in his home. It belonged to his mother, but it was more ornamental, like the statutes of Christ, the Virgin Mary, and the saints that were all around their house. They were about a foot tall, like the G.I. Joe dolls he used to play with when he was a little boy. There weren't Bibles in church, only hymnals and missals. His mother's Bible was placed on her dresser in his parents' bedroom, along with her favorite statues. It was her own altar, and she used to pray before it every day, saying the Rosary before they went to mass. Gio never understood the Rosary but was fascinated by his mother's methodical handling of her beads as she prayed in silence or softly as if she were whispering to God.

Gio started walking through the aisles of books, and Alex quickly decided to offer his assistance, like he would with any other inmate. He quickly prayed, took in some focusing breaths, and approached.

"Good morning, Mr. Bruno."

"Good morning. You can call me Gio. And your name is Alex, right?"

"Yes, Alex Martinez."

"Right. How could I forget?"

In that moment, both men were thinking about the 800-pound gorilla in the room. The prophetic word of knowledge God had given Alex for Gio. But they weren't going there today. That was for another time.

"Can I help you find something?"

"Yes. I've decided to read the Bible."

A small smile broke out on Alex's face, and he nodded his head in affirmation.

"Excellent choice. I recommend the New International Version. I think it offers the most direct translation."

Gio thought, *Okay, there are different versions and translations, whatever that's about.*

"Okay. I'm sure whatever you recommend is fine."

"Why don't you have a seat in one of the booths and I'll bring you a Bible."

Gio sat in the middle of a row of several booths. There were only a few other inmates in the library. A couple were sitting in booths at the far end of the row, and others were sitting at some tables in the center of the room. Both Gio and Alex were aware of their audience. Alex brought Gio a large, leather-bound Bible, with the words New International Version Study Bible imprinted on the reddish-brown cover.

"Here you go, Mr. Bruno. A lot of guys have questions about how to start reading the Bible. This is a study version that offers information on the geography and history. I believe the Bible is meant to be read like any other book. You start at the beginning and read through to the end."

"Thank you, I appreciate your help."

Gio opened the book and began to read "In the beginning, God created the heavens and the earth."

Gio continued to go to the library every day and read the Bible. The study Bible was helpful, but he still took notes on his thoughts and questions. He was searching for answers. Alex asked him a couple of times if he wished to take the Bible back to his cell, but he declined. He wanted to be close to Alex. He felt drawn to him. He wanted a reason to keep returning to the library.

Gio was keenly observant during the weekly Bible study and prayer meeting Alex led. There were several men, and it was a mixed group: young, old, Black, Hispanic, and White. Meeting space was limited so the library had to suffice, and there had to be two COs for coverage.

The meetings were held in an enclosed room with a large sliding glass door. Gio couldn't hear the conversations, but he could see the men. Alex was engaging as usual, but they were all engaged. Gio watched them having intense conversations. At times it looked as if they were all agreeing, at least all of them were nodding their heads. At other times it looked like a debate was going on, one or another of the men would be holding up his Bible, as if for emphasis, and reading. There was plenty of laughter and some tears. At times all the men in the group would come around one, place their hands on him and appear to be praying, or at least providing encouraging words. But always, at the end of the meeting, the men would stand around in a circle, join hands, bow their heads, and pray. The only prayer Gio knew was the Our Father. He had never memorized the Hail Mary when he was in school, but when he found out it wasn't in the Bible, he didn't feel bad about it.

As the weeks passed, Alex began checking in with Gio to see if he needed anything or had any questions. Gio had many, and they began discussing the Bible and getting to know each other. But there was always that 800-pound gorilla between them, that prophetic word of knowledge. Slowly, over time, Alex began ministering to Gio, explaining how God had changed his life. He eventually shared how he had received a word of knowledge from Hector, his former cellmate, through which God had opened the door to his heart.

He couldn't tell him, but Gio started feeling sorry for Alex. Here he was, living this life of hope, and it was all a lie. He was no different than himself—he was a murderer who had committed a mortal sin. In fact, he was in a worse situation. Gio had accepted his fate, but here was Alex believing that he was going to heaven, and it was a lie. He was going to hell.

Alex had made a habit of inviting Gio to join the Bible study. He practiced the broken-record technique. It had always worked for him in the past. People would either agree with whatever he was proposing or tell him to stop asking because it was never going to happen. Either way, he would get closure.

One day Gio caught him by surprise when he finally accepted. Alex knew that Gio had been watching the group. They would even make eye contact on occasion during the meetings. They were getting to know each other's moods and mannerisms. It didn't happen every day, but Gio came to recognize Alex's shift in body language when he was about to extend the invite. He would start nodding his head, ever so slightly, start picking up books for reshelving—a sign that he was preparing to disengage—then take a deep breath in through his nose and exhale through his mouth. Alex was trying to think of a graceful way to extend the invite when Gio said,

"I've decided to accept your invitation to join the group."

"That's great. Ah, well, you obviously know when and where we meet." That crease of a smile broke out on Alex's face.

"Yeah, I got it. I'll see you there."

The group was illuminating for Gio. He could see how God was using it to impact the men who came. He and Alex were the only lifers, and he thought it ironic how God could use a man who was heading to hell to minister to others. But one thing he had learned through his reading of the Bible was that God could use all things. And the deliverance he saw happening was real.

During one meeting, a young man, Juan, was obviously seething. There was always the element of violence in Big Sandy, the potential for injury and death. There was a darkness that hung in the air, looking to devour those who were receptive and vulnerable. When there was an incident, the prison would be placed on lockdown, which could last for a week or two until investigations had been completed. And word would get around. An inmate had recently been stabbed to death in the yard, gutted, and left with his intestines spilling onto the pavement.

Juan was 23, doing time for armed robbery. He wasn't in a gang. He was an addict, a customer, not a good recruit. He would lie, cheat, and steal from anyone, including his own mother, to get what he needed to get high. He was a young Christian, a baby if you will, but he was being healed.

No one in the group knew that the inmate who had been murdered was Juan's childhood friend. This was the first meeting since the lockdown, and there was a heavy darkness over him that had to be addressed. After opening in prayer, Alex spoke to Juan.

"What's happening with you, Juan?"

Juan started breathing heavily, staring straight ahead.

"Juan, what's going on?"

Juan balled up his fists and started rocking back and forth, still staring with a distant angry blindness in his eyes.

"Juan, God is with us. When two or more are gathered in his name, he is in the midst of them. Let it go; let us help you."

"They killed Jose! They gutted him like a pig! I saw his guts poured out on the yard. And for nothing, some bullshit on the outs!"

Alex stood up and stepped toward Juan, who began shouting.

"I'm going to kill them! I'm going to kill them! I'm going to kill them!"

The COs covering the library were up and approaching the room. Alex saw them, raised his hand, and they stopped and stood near the door. Alex then kneeled in front of Juan, placed his left hand on Juan's knee and reached his right hand around the back of Juan's neck. Juan was still rocking and began hyperventilating. Alex brought his forehead to rest against Juan's forehead and began speaking softly.

"It's alright, brother. God has this. He is here with us. Vengeance is mine says the Lord. We are to forgive, as he has forgiven us."

Juan started shaking uncontrollably and wailing. Alex wrapped his arms around him and began to pray.

"Lord, I pray your healing hand upon Juan right now. Heal his broken heart, Lord, and give him the strength to forgive as you have forgiven us. Give him the strength to stand in your service, Lord, and not succumb to the enemy who wants to destroy him."

A couple of the other men in the group got up, stood next to Juan, and placed their hands on his shoulders. They also began to pray. The entire hour was spent in prayer for Juan and before it was over, he was at peace, exhausted, but at peace. Alex closed in prayer for Jose's family and asked for justice.

The assailant was arrested and indicted for capital murder. Juan continued to receive his healing and grew closer to the Lord.

Chapter 13

GIO WAS AMAZED AT what he had witnessed and how God was using Alex, another lost soul like himself. He was compelled to tell Alex the truth. Alex was feeling the conviction of the Holy Spirit each time he saw Gio. Life was too short, especially in Big Sandy. They were drawn together like magnets and alone in the library that day, but for the two COs on duty.

"Can we talk?" Alex asked Gio.

"Sure."

Gio sensed an opportunity arising to get to the heart of the matter and maybe hear a word of wisdom from God. Alex asked the COs if it was okay if he and Gio went into the meeting room for a little privacy, and they agreed.

Alex was confident this was the moment ordained by God and knew only one way to go about it—straight for the heart.

"Gio, it's been great studying the Bible with you, and you have been a blessing to us all, but I have to ask you a question."

"Yeah, what's that?"

"Have you ever asked Jesus to come into your heart?"

Gio paused, looked at Alex, and took a deep breath.

"No. It's not something God wants to hear from me."

"What are you talking about, Gio? Christ went to the cross for us all to be forgiven."

"Not for me and not for you either. We are murderers and committed a mortal sin."

Alex was taken aback. He had heard many men profess their unworthiness because of their sins, but this was a pronounced declaration, and he found himself struggling for the words.

"What?! That's not the word of God. Look at all the murderers in the Bible that were used by God, like Moses and King David. David would've been indicted for murder for hire today."

Gio had studied his Bible and felt prepared for this discussion.

"That's Old Testament, Alex. God also ordered the Israelites to wipe out entire cities, including innocent women and children. Where's the love in that?"

Both men felt their hearts pounding and their adrenaline flowing.

"But Christ went to the cross for our sins; even the thief on the cross next to him received salvation."

"But the guy on the other cross, a murderer, didn't bother to ask for forgiveness because he knew he had committed a mortal sin!"

Alex was at a loss. He wasn't good at debating scripture, especially reconciling the Old Testament with the New. All he knew was you had to have faith, and all he could do was fall on God's word.

"Romans 10:9 says that if you confess with your mouth that Christ is Lord and believe in your heart that he was raised from the dead, you will be saved. That's all there is to it, Gio."

Gio hadn't thought about his mother's ghost in almost two years, but Alex's word took him back to the SHU, in his cell that morning and her words, "Romani dieci, nove . . . Romani dieci, nove . . . Romani dieci, nove."

And he began to repeat them.

"Romani dieci, nove . . . Romani dieci, nove . . . Romani dieci, nove."

Alex just sat there and watched Gio become undone, drop his face to the table and weep, still muttering,

"Romani dieci, nove . . . Romani dieci, nove . . . Romani dieci, nove."

"Gio, what are you saying? What does that mean?"

"Romans 10:9," Gio managed to whisper through his heaving sobs.

"My mama came to me in the hole and spoke those words to me."

Alex sat still and just watched Gio cry. Finally, he asked, "Gio, do you want to pray?"

And when Gio spoke, it was like God whispering to him, "Yes."

"Just repeat after me," Alex said, and let God use him to lead Gio into the Kingdom.

Chapter 14

GIO HAD SURRENDERED TO Christ.

He felt immeasurable joy and began to see how God had been working in his life, especially through his Mama. He knew he had been saved by her prayers, but he was like a child in his faith. There was so much for him to learn, and he was eager to grow in the Word. He continued to attend Alex's Bible study and men's prayer group. He no longer cared about the outside world and became focused on scripture.

He told Gio Jr. to cancel his subscription to the New York Times, and so he missed the article about Paul Danbury's successful campaign for mayor of Providence. Gio had never been a big fan of watching TV, so he also missed the story on the news. To humble himself before God, he took a job on the maintenance crew. Low man on the totem pole, his glamorous position involved emptying the trash and cleaning restrooms. He started taking a couple of courses offered through the local community college, English Composition and Abnormal Psychology. But his primary focus was growing in his faith and prayer life.

The group grew to a dozen men, which Alex said was the maximum number to still have meaningful interaction. He also liked the number because Jesus had twelve disciples. One of the things Gio marveled at was how the scripture they read was applicable to their daily lives which were constantly filled with temptation. Often the group spent half their time discussing specific situations and circumstances one or more of the men were going through, sometimes having to do with family. These family situations were extremely painful at times and brought up feelings of guilt and helplessness. But they would always pray that God change the narrative. There was power there, and they all felt it if they were open to it. They all came to know the verse, in Matthew 18:20, "For where two or three gather in my name, there I am with them." They were twelve and prayed that God magnify his presence among them.

Gio no longer had dreams about his mother but would have a sense of colors when he woke, as if he had dreamed about her. That sense would quickly dissipate once he began moving through his day.

Those colors returned to him the day he walked into a classroom to empty the trash and met Greta Jones. The room was new to his route, and he was somewhat surprised when he walked into splashes of red, green, yellow, and blue on canvases capturing works in progress. For a second, he had a déjà vu moment of waking up with colors on his mind.

He had noticed the CO in the hallway outside the room but didn't see Greta Jones sitting quietly at a corner desk, writing something in a notebook. Greta was a 62-year-old high school art teacher from Ashland, Kentucky, retired after 30 years. Her husband died from a heart attack ten years earlier. He was a foreman at the Unity Aluminum Rolling Mill. Their only son died from a heroin overdose five years after that. They told her it was the fentanyl that really killed him. He had been in and out of prison for several years prior to his death. Since retirement, Greta had spent more time at church, going to the midweek prayer meeting and volunteering at the soup kitchen. She knew God had healed her through her art after suffering through loss and felt called to start a ministry for those lost souls in prison, like her son.

Greta saw Gio walk into the room and could tell that he hadn't seen her. He was just standing there, staring at the canvasses. She got up from her seat and began to approach, while offering her hand.

"Hello."

"Oh, hello. I'm so sorry. I didn't mean to barge in on you."

Gio noticed the woman had a firm handshake.

"That's fine. I saw you were looking at the paintings."

"Yes, the colors are beautiful."

"Yes, they are. Have you ever done any painting?"

"Me? No. I've never even drawn a stick figure."

"Well, you're welcome to join the class."

"Oh, I don't know ma'am. Like I said, I've never even drawn a stick figure. I've never even thought about art or paintings, or anything like that."

"It's Greta if you please, Greta Jones. And what's your name?"

"Giordano Bruno, but people call me Gio."

"Nice to meet you, Gio."

"Nice to meet you, ma'am . . . I mean Greta."

"Well, you don't need to have any experience, but it helps if you have an interest in art. You just have to be open to it, and I'll help you. That's why I'm here. Will you at least think about it?" Greta asked.

"Ok. I'll think about it."

The CO started clearing his throat, signaling Gio that it was time to move on.

"I've got to go. Nice meeting you, Greta."

"Nice meeting you, Gio. I hope to see you in class."

He nodded at Greta as he emptied the trash and left the room.

The night after he met Greta, Gio had another dream about his mother, but this time they weren't at daily mass together. He was only six; it was toward the end of summer, and she was working in her garden around dusk, bent down on her right knee. Rays from the lowering sun were slicing through the trees, leaving golden beams across her back as he approached. She was wearing a yellow house dress and was working on her tomato plants, picking the ripe fruit to place in her wicker basket on the ground. Yellow was their favorite color. The birds were singing as Gio tried to sneak up on her. He reached out and just before he was able to touch her shoulder, she swung around on one knee, and said,

"Amore mio, Gio mio! Don't you remember? I have eyes in the back of my head!" They embraced, and Gio felt the warmth from the golden rays of the sun reaching through his mama, filling him up. They stood up and started laughing together as she picked up her basket of tomatoes.

And Gio was still consumed by the colors of her yellow dress, the red tomatoes, her brownish red hair, olive skin, and brown eyes when he woke up. He could see her still, as if she were standing in front of him, not like her ghost, but a picture in his mind. Her picture stayed with him for a long time.

It became a new recurring dream and each time, it was more vivid. Gio rearranged his schedule so he could be in the art room when the men were there working on their paintings.

Greta started each class by saying, "Art is a gift from God through which he can create a path to healing." Gio chatted with Greta a few times and learned that although she worked and taught many forms of expression, oil was her favorite. It had more history, and, in Greta's opinion, offered the most creative possibilities.

Over time, stepping into the room was like stepping into another world for Gio. It wasn't just the colors and the smell of the paint, it was the passion and purpose, the freedom offered through the canvas. And it was Greta, in whom he saw kindness and love, but also a distant sadness in her eyes.

Gio prayed for Greta and the men in her class. He prayed that a healing come through the expression of love. He also prayed that he receives God's plan for his life. And when he thought about God during the day, he saw his mother, tending to her garden, wrapped in yellow, brightened by the sun, reaching into the green plants, and pulling forth bright red tomatoes with droplets of morning dew that glistened like stars. And through it all, he heard God calling him to Greta's class. He decided to become one of her students.

On his first day, Greta decided to start at the beginning since there were a couple of other new students in addition to Gio. She explained that one of the most important fundamentals of oil painting is light and shadow, referred to as tonal value, or value. She taught that tonal value is even more important than color—if your color is beautiful but your values are not right then your painting won't work. However, if your colors are bad but your values are right on, then your painting will work. So, focusing more on tonal value than color is a good idea when starting out.

Gio didn't fully understand the lesson, but he did know light and shadow, good and evil; this he did know. Greta showed a video that set forth the steps, sketching an outline, then selecting and mixing colors. They also viewed a slide show of some of the masterpieces, great works of art, in addition to some of Greta's paintings and those of her students.

The following week the new students began their projects. The moment Gio sat down on the stool, he saw his mother in all her glory on the white canvas. And without thinking about what he was doing, he began to draw, following the lines of what he saw.

He was completely absorbed. The voices around him faded to the point of being barely audible, and he saw a shining orb around his work. Gio was unaware that halfway through the class, Greta and the other students had stopped what there were doing and were watching him. And before the hour was over, his mama's image was fully captured, as he had dreamed of her, as he had been with her when he was a young boy. As Gio was finishing, he heard Greta calling his name, "Gio, Gio, Gio . . ." And he was back with them. He looked at Greta.

"Ms. Jones, I mean, Greta?"

"Gio, Gio, that's amazing," Greta said, as the COs began to call out instructions to the men and led them from the room. Greta sat on the stool in front of Gio's drawing and just marveled at it. And then she remembered the scripture she had read during her daily devotional that morning. She got up and went to her backpack. She took out her Bible and opened it to where she had marked it earlier. And she started reading Exodus 31 for the second time that day, stopped at verses 3 and 4 and reread,

". . . and I have filled him with the Spirit of God, with wisdom, with understanding, with knowledge and with all kinds of skills to make artistic designs . . ." And she thought, *this is a miracle.*

During the next class, Greta continued her lesson for the new students on drawing their sketches, then spent time with Gio explaining the use of color again, all for the purpose of achieving strong tonal value. He listened attentively and even jotted down a few notes, and then went to spend time with his mother.

Just like before, she appeared within the canvas; they were embraced by the Holy Spirit, and he began to paint. He worked at a frenetic pace, stroking his brushes across the canvas with all the colors of that moment in time. The class was an hour long, and like before, the sounds and voices in the room became distant to him, almost inaudible, like he was under water. Halfway through the class, everyone in the room had stopped what they were doing and were watching Gio work. Even the COs were looking in amazement.

By the end of the hour the portrait was complete; his mother, face forward, walking away from her garden, framed by tall stalks of corn and sunflowers the same color as her favorite yellow dress, three rays of morning light reaching down through the web of branches in the tall trees: one landing on her head, lighting her beautiful brown, smiling face; one covering her right foot; the third a step ahead, spotlighting her basket filled with yellow corn, ripe red tomatoes, green grapes, and dark olives hanging over the edges.

Chapter 15

It took twenty-five years for Agent Taurino to arrive at that small moment, when his decisions would alter the course of many lives. During that quarter century, key changes had occurred.

Gio was divorced from his wife during his first year of imprisonment. He didn't blame her. He had lied to her and many other family members and friends. He prayed for forgiveness. He missed his wife. He missed the intimacy. But it helped him to focus more on the Lord. He came to see it as a daily sacrifice, like the thorn in Paul's side. Three times Paul had prayed to the Lord to remove the thorn, but God allowed it to remain.

Gio thought about Paul a lot when wrestling with the isolation within his own flesh. The beginning of Chapter 7 of 1 Corinthians spoke to him when Paul said, "It is good for man not to have sexual relations with a woman," as well at the end of the Chapter, where he says, "I wish that all of you were as I am."

Gio was a model inmate and continued to paint.

During the time he was at Big Sandy, Greta Jones just stepped back and bathed in the blessing of God's Glory. She continued to teach her students and would often lecture while Gio worked, explaining his brush techniques and use of color. Word spread within the Bureau of Prisons. Administration and psych staff came to Big Sandy to observe. Some suggested that he was a late-blooming prodigy, or simply a freak of nature. But Greta knew otherwise. She knew of his faith, a faith they shared.

During the ten years Gio was at Big Sandy, they had often discussed God and the Bible. They prayed together and got to know each other. They prayed for one another and for the students in her class. Greta had read stories about blessed objects that brought healing. She found a few online and, in her mind, they all traced back to one of her favorite stories in the Bible in Luke Chapter 8, when a lady who had been suffering from hemorrhages for twelve years came up behind Jesus, touched the hem of his cloak, and was healed through her faith.

Greta had seen such healing occur in Big Sandy. Sometimes Gio would dream about an inmate, paint what he saw, and offer it to the man. In every case, it brought some form of healing. At other times, inmates would bring Gio photos of family members in hopes he would paint a portrait. There were many requests, and Gio had to work on smaller canvases. In her classes, after receiving a portrait painted by Gio, Greta saw men being baptized in the Holy Spirit and washed clean by their own tears.

She also heard about other men being healed throughout Big Sandy. Inmates from other institutions, having heard about Gio, would have their families send in photos. He would paint these portraits, and Greta would take them home and later mail them to the families. She maintained contact with the families and heard numerous stories of healing.

When Greta finally brought her favorite photo of her husband and son to Gio, he said, "What took you so long?" She knew her husband was saved but had doubts about her son.

She had watched Gio paint many times and it was always the same: his frenetic pace, with perfection, like he was in a trance. To Greta, it was like God was painting through him.

Gio was permitted to have some oil paints in his cell, and he would occasionally work there. He painted the portrait of Greta's husband and son while in his cell. When he handed her the painting that afternoon, she took it in her hands and sat down.

As she studied the lines and colors, the faces of her men, she felt a warmth spread throughout her body, starting in her fingertips, and spreading through her hands, her arms, her entire body, coming to rest and dwell in her mind and her heart. She had never felt anything like it. She had never been baptized in the Holy Spirit. It was like waves in the ocean, washing over her again and again. When she could no longer see the painting through her tears, she began to touch it with her fingers and kiss it, feeling the texture of the paint. And waves of love kept washing over her. She was lost in time.

She then felt hands resting on her shoulder and heard Gio's voice, "Greta . . . Greta, we have to go."

Greta turned and saw Gio standing behind her. The rest of her students were gone. She stood up and they embraced, "Thank you Gio, thank you for letting God use you."

Gio's time in prison was well spent. Even though his artistic ability was anointed by God, he studied with Greta and learned art history, techniques, therapeutic principles, and was certified in art therapy by the time he was transferred from Big Sandy. He also earned bachelor's degrees in Art and Design, and Biblical Studies.

He was first transferred to the Federal Correctional Institution (FCI) Ray Brook, a medium-security facility in Ray Brook, New York, then FCI Fort Dix, a low-security facility in New Jersey. Gio continued to paint and was asked to paint murals on the walls of these facilities once the administration realized the extent of his gift. He was also permitted to teach art therapy, and many inmates received healings as well as some correctional officers.

Gio was a model inmate and mentor to many men, and the prison administrators saw a dramatic impact on the reduction of disciplinary incidents with the men whose lives he touched. He continued to run Bible studies and led numerous men to Christ.

Gio's final stay within the Bureau of Prisons was at The Federal Medical Center Fort Devens in Ayers, Massachusetts. He had spent over twenty years imprisoned and was in his mid-60s. Now that he was closer to home, Gio Jr. was able to visit him regularly.

It was always a great blessing for both, as they spent time sharing testimonies and talking about God.

During this time, Paul Danbury had served as the Mayor of Providence. When he came into office in 1992, there had been fifty murders in the city that year, making Providence the murder capital of American cities with a population of 200,000 or less. There was corruption within the police department, and the city was on the verge of bankruptcy.

During his first four-year term, Danbury had cleaned up the police department and hired 100 new officers, fulfilling his campaign promise of getting tough on crime and cleaning up the garbage. He had also worked closely with the state treasurer and city clerk. By the end of his second term, they had assembled a top-notch group of financial experts and pulled the city out of bankruptcy.

Danbury and his wife, Susan, now had two children, a boy and a girl, ages 12 and 10. Susan hadn't achieved full professorship at Brown but had become the chair of her department, which offered her more flexibility and allowed time for the kids. Paul's political career had become the centerpiece of their marriage.

Paul had always felt somewhat entitled, a character flaw instilled by his parents, but his sense of entitlement only grew with his success. He was praised by his constituents as the "Savior of Providence," and during his campaign for a fourth term in office, he ran uncontested.

That same year, he was named by *The Washington Post* as one of the top-50 mayors in the country. There was talk of the governor's office and beyond. Providence was thriving, and there were huge opportunities for real estate and business developers. The voters had approved funding for the construction of a minor league ballpark and an arena on the outskirts of downtown. Inspired by this success, Paul traveled to New York City several times and met with Donald Trump to discuss the possibility of a casino in Providence.

Agent Taurino took notice when the contracts for the ballpark and arena were awarded to the Giattino brothers, successful land developers from Cranston. They were second- generation Italians whose great-grandparents were from Northern Italy. It was known by law enforcement that they were associated with the Patriarca Family and paid to play as far as union contracts with the concrete and trucking industries were concerned.

Taurino knew that Gio had dealt with the Giattinos on behalf of the family over the years, and there was still a close relationship between them. Working with the BOP, John had learned that there had been several phone calls over the years between Gio and Vincent Giattino, the older brother, and regular visits once Gio was transferred to the Tri-State area. Taurino decided that a second visit with Gio was warranted. John still harbored guilt in his heart about lying to Gio and putting him in the SHU for a year. In addition to talking with him about the Giattinos, he needed to apologize and hoped that Gio would forgive him.

This visit was in stark contrast to the first. Rather than walking down the endless halls of Big Sandy, John was escorted to an open outside area with picnic tables. Gio was housed at the satellite camp adjacent to the medical facility. It was a beautiful, sunny spring day. Agent Taurino couldn't help hearing the birds singing and seeing the deep blue sky framing the budding Japanese Maples.

Gio was sitting at one of the tables. There was no one else in the area. Taurino could see that Gio was healthy. He looked like he had gained about twenty pounds of muscle; his skin was dark brown from spending time out in the sun, and his hair was full, neatly combed and graying around the ears. Taurino sat down directly across from Gio, and the CO stepped far enough away to give them plenty of privacy.

"Agent Taurino, how are you? It's been a long time. You look the same."

"How are you? You look great. You've obviously been working out."

"In the gym and the garden."

Agent Taurino took a deep breath.

"Gio, I came here to apologize."

"For what?"

"We lied to the warden at Big Sandy about evidence of a conspiracy to murder you. We thought a hit would be coming, but it never happened. Apparently, your historic declarations in court that day did not offend the family as we anticipated. We also figured out that your father's legacy left you untouchable. It was a complete fabrication. This is no longer your father's mafia. Things have changed."

Taurino paused and took another deep breath. He felt relieved. He had been thinking about this day for a long time. It had kept him up many a night.

Gio looked at Taurino with a slight grin on his face while subtly nodding his head in understanding. The two men were transfixed for a few minutes, which seemed like an eternity to Agent Taurino. He didn't know what to think.

"That's it?" Gio asked.

Taurino continued to look at Gio and studied him for a moment. He looked calm, at peace, sincere. Taurino continued in a sheepish tone of voice.

"Ah, that's why you were placed in the SHU."

"Best thing that ever happened to me!"

"What?! You've got to be kidding me!"

"John. May I call you John?"

"Ah . . . sure."

"I knew it was a lie. I still have friends in Rhode Island, you know."

"Um, yeah. I know you do."

"Listen, John. If you came here asking for forgiveness you've got it.

I forgave you and Danbury years ago. Have you ever heard the verse from the Bible, Romans 8:28?"

"No. I can't say that I have."

"Well, it says, 'And we know that in all things God works for the good of those who love him, who have been called according to his purpose.'"

John sat still, clearly caught off guard. This was not the same man he had investigated.

"I don't know what to say."

"You don't have to say anything. Just know that you are forgiven."

They again sat in silence, looking directly into each other's eyes.

John was trying to figure out what to say next. He had rehearsed this moment in his mind dozens of times since he started investigating the Danbury Administration. He knew if he could solicit Gio's help, the case would be rock solid. But he was captured by the change in this man. He knew him to be an uncompromising hit man, an old-school mafioso who was not willing to rat on his friends. He felt that his performance at sentencing was just a show for his family. He had to admit that it was an incredible feat for Gio to live the life without his family really knowing the full extent of his involvement. He was clearly an intelligent man. But there was no anger in him that John could see. Gio seemed almost joyful.

Gio looked at this man whom he thought of often during the past twenty-some-odd years. He remembered John had an unbalanced obsession about his job, but he was honest until the end. He thought it must've been very difficult for him to go along with Danbury's lies.

Gio tried to silence his thoughts and hear from God. He found all his direction from God's Word and would start this process by reciting the verse in his mind that spoke directly into this struggle: *"We demolish all arguments and every pretension that sets itself up against the knowledge of God and we take captive every thought to make it obedient to Christ." 2 Corinthians 10:5.* As Gio was meditating on the second half of the verse, he was interrupted by John's voice.

"I really came to ask for your help."

"Why do you need my help?"

"I think you know. You're a smart guy. I'm sure you've already figured it out." Gio thought for a moment about how to respond. He knew John was talking about the Danbury case, but he wanted to be sure.

"I don't know if you've checked with the warden, but I have disconnected from the outside. I don't read the paper anymore or watch the news. I'm a Christian now, and the only thing I listen to on the radio is worship music. My focus in here is painting and teaching art therapy. I'm afraid you're going to have to spell it out for me, John."

John had checked with the warden and had read Gio's file. The only way he knew to go about this was straight ahead.

"Gio, I know you're still close to the Giattino brothers, and Vinny has visited you regularly since you got back to the East Coast. I believe he told you that they were awarded the contracts by Danbury to build the ballpark and arena in Downtown Providence."

John paused and studied Gio's face. He looked like he was thinking. He continued.

"Nobody wants to talk to us right now, but I believe that Danbury received a huge kickback from your friends. The local contractors know it as well but they're afraid to say anything. It's a double-edged sword for them. They don't want to be shut out of the transfer stations, and they need to get those smaller-city jobs."

"I see. I see you've got a lot on your mind. But how are you, John? Are you married, any kids?"

"Not married, no kids but I do have a girlfriend."

"That's great. How long have you been together?"

"Ten years."

"What's her name? . . . What does she do? . . . How'd you meet?"

John realized that Gio had quickly taken over the conversation. Under ordinary circumstances he would redirect his subject. But Gio's voice was somehow soothing to him. He felt the warmth of the sun on the back of his neck, a gentle breeze across his face, the birds singing, and a warmth from the man sitting across from him. He felt like he could tell Gio his life story. But suddenly the scene from the movie *Moonlight* flashed across his mind, when Cher slaps Nicholas Cage across the face while saying, "Snap out of it!" And he did and began to redirect.

"Gio, we're not here to talk about me, but thank you for your interest. We're here to talk about whether you want to help your friends or not."

"I am devoted to God and my friends," Gio said.

"I know that. I've seen your prison record. I've read about all the good work you've done during your time."

"So, what exactly are you talking about, John?"

"The Giattinos. They're going down. But you can help make for a safer landing."

At that moment, the CO started clearing his throat and held up the five fingers of his right hand, directing that they had five minutes left on their visit. John was out of the box, out of his comfort zone. His visit with Gio had been unsettling. He didn't know if he'd have another shot at this and began to ramble a bit.

"Gio, do you know what misprision of a felony is?" John asked, then thought, Wait a minute. I didn't come here to make any threats. I'm blowing it.

"You know I was born and raised Roman Catholic, just like you."

"Yes, we do share the same religion," Gio said.

"And . . . and . . ." and for the first time John could remember, he didn't know what to say.

"And what I have found is a relationship with God through Christ. It has nothing to do with religion," Gio said.

"Ok, fellas. The visit's over," one CO said as the officers approached the table.

"You can come with me, counselor," the second CO said.

Gio and John stood up and began to shake hands.

"Well . . . well, why don't you see what your Bible tells you to do and pray about it," John said.

"That's a good idea. I'll do that."

"Can I visit you again?

"I don't know. I'll have to pray about it."

The sky had been clear during his early morning drive to Devans but was overcast and ominous when he started the drive back. Rain drops began splashing off the windshield as John started beating himself up mentally during the drive back to Rhode Island. He had always felt deep guilt about lying to Gio and wanted to make amends somehow.

He thought that by giving Gio a chance to help him nail Danbury, there would be some restorative justice. He'd have to go back again, and soon. He didn't think Gio would refuse his visit. He was just joking at the end. John's mind was a flurry of what ifs, should've's, whys and what's nexts, but it cleared when a bright ray of sunshine suddenly broke through the clouds. He was driving south on I-95 when the beam shot through. Its light created a ring of colors in the surrounding clouds . . . purple, pink, dark blue. John thought it was 'magnificent,' one of his grandmother's favorite words.

He hadn't thought about that word since he was a child. He also hadn't confessed since he made his Confirmation. He started thinking about Gio, his life in prison, his peace, his light. What had he said, Romans 8 something? John had never read the Bible, only the Missal when he went to church with his parents. Maybe he would read Romans.

He had seen defendants get jailhouse religion, but it was like the icing on their sentencing performance before the judge or the parole board. But Gio had been living this life for over twenty years. He was not the same man they had tried in the early 90s. John knew that prison changed people. He had seen it. It made them worse. But Gio was different.

The week following his visit, John discussed case strategy with one of the assistant U.S. attorneys assigned to the case. He liked William Chin, even though Bill was a Millennial, or at least John thought he was. He couldn't keep up with these generational definitions.

Bill was a hard-working prosecutor, respectful and willing to learn. From spending time with him in his office and studying the walls, John knew he was a graduate of UCONN Law School, which he appreciated. He had had enough of dealing with lawyers on both sides with degrees from Yale, Harvard, or some other Ivy

League school. To John, these attorneys were often know-it-alls who thought they had all the answers before asking any questions.

Bill was a rising star in the U.S. Attorney's Office and being on the Danbury team was both a test and a feather in his cap. Part of Bill's training was for him to work with the FBI in developing the investigation, obtaining, and organizing the Government's evidence. John often worked with younger attorneys. He knew from the higher-ups that part of his mission was to train new lawyers.

They met in Bill's office. Bill was 25 and looked the part. He stood about 5'7", weighed a fit 165 pounds (During one of their first meetings, they spent most of the time talking about lifting weights), had black hair, perfectly cut with a part slightly to the right, and a pleasant face with a strong, squared-off jaw. He had agreed with John that a visit to Devans was a good idea. He greeted John cheerfully as he walked into the office.

"Good morning, John. How was the visit?"

"I'm not really sure. He sort of caught me off guard."

"What do you mean?"

"I don't know exactly. It's hard to describe. He told me he had forgiven me and Danbury years ago."

The fact of how he and Danbury had conspired against Gio was known only to John, Paul, and now Gio.

"Well, that's nice. That's a good beginning. We've learned that he's built an impressive record while imprisoned. I guess he's 'rehabilitated.' Ha-ha, if that's still the term."

"I tell you, Bill. This was for real. Nobody can pull off a scam for twenty years. He's not the same man. I'm sure of it."

"Well, that's great news. Is he going to help us? I would bet that he's chomping at the bit to get back at Danbury."

"I'm not so sure about that. I mean, there's this peace about him. He teaches art therapy for Christ's sake, literally! I don't know if he'd want to get involved."

"I'm hoping he would if he understood that we will bring him back to court for a reduced sentence under Rule 35," Bill said.

"I didn't get that far," John said.

"Ok. No worries. You'll be going back, yeah?"

"Yeah. For sure. But I'm not sure what to expect."

"Well, ok. You prep your team, and we'll meet this Friday at 9:00 am to make sure we've dotted all our i's and crossed all our t's. Does that work for you, John?"

Both men stood up and shook hands.

"This is my only case. 9:00 on Friday works for me, boss."

John left and as Bill sat back down behind his desk, a small smile broke out on his face as he thought, *he called me boss.*

When John arrived at Bill's office that Friday morning, he found three neatly arranged documents on his desk. Many of the assistants he had worked with over the years were like whirlwinds, and their offices made them look like hoarders, with boxes of evidence here and there and stacks of documents scattered about. Bill was organized, which made John feel like they were kindred souls. He knew that IT had something to do with it. Everything was electronic these days, but still, the kid was organized. Bill stood up from behind his desk as John entered the office and greeted him warmly, as usual.

"Agent Taurino. Welcome to my laboratory."

They shook hands.

"Counselor. Always a pleasure."

They sat down.

"Ok. So, the first document on your left is the arrest warrant for Danbury, the second are the search and seizure warrants for his home and office, and the two-pager on the right is the target letter for the Giattinos. I want you to take your time and review them before we launch Project Nor'easter on Sunday morning. My office is yours for as long as you need."

"I don't think it will take very long," John said, as he picked up the lengthy warrant applications.

"You know, Bill, I listened to 100 hours of calls on Danbury. My favorites are his conversations with Trump, trying to persuade him to build a casino."

"I know. We've all heard of an ass-kisser, but Danbury has raised the art to a new level. He's an asshole licker."

Both men chuckled and John shook his head.

"But you know what the most revealing thing is?"

What's that?" Bill replied.

"In all those calls, you know how many times he mentioned his wife and kids?"

Bill stared at John, knowingly nodding his head.

"Zero, zilch. Bill, they're just trappings, like his Armani suits and BMWs!"

"The guy's so smart that he's stupid. What's he thinking on a 150K annual

salary?" Bill asked rhetorically. "I appreciate his greed and arrogance," he added, "It makes for a more compelling case."

The plan was set: an early-morning visit to the mayor's home on Sunday to execute the warrants, followed by target letters to the Giattinos. John was organizing the assignments for his agents on the team when he received a call from Bill.

"Good morning, Bill."

"Good morning, John. How's it going?"

"I'm almost done. I'll email the plan to you by noon."

"Excellent. And after the arrests, we'll have the target letters sent to Gio's pals, hand-delivered by a couple of agents of your choice."

"I'll send the two rooks. They'll get a kick out of it."

"And then you can make another trip to see Gio. Tell him you found Jesus and that Jesus told you he should cooperate."

"It's no joke, counselor. He's not the same guy."

"I believe it, John. That's why I'm hoping he'll help us with this case."

"Bill, you don't understand. The first thing he said to me when we met was that he has forgiven me and Danbury for what we did to him!"

"Okay. I get it. His motivation isn't revenge. So, we go at it from two angles. First, he's helping himself by getting out early as a reward for his cooperation, and second, he's helping his friends by encouraging them to cooperate so that they receive lighter sentences."

"It's worth the effort," John said, and added, "It's the least I can do, after the pressure we put on him to cooperate against the Patriarcas."

"Exactly."

"Well okay, Counselor, I'll finish up with the search plan and email them today, and I'll see you at the staging site before the sun rises this Sunday."

"Just one more thing John, before we hang up."

"What's that?"

"You know the Bureau of Prisons is part of the DOJ."

"And I know you're only three years out of law school, Counselor. Get to the point."

"Right. To the point. The FBI has the authority to conduct investigations within the BOP . . ."

"Right. The point, Bill. Get to the point!" John had uncharacteristically lost his patience with Bill.

"Well, if Gio welcomes a visit from one of the Giattinos, most likely Vinny—that's who he's closest to, right?—we place a small microphone under the table and hope for the best."

"What the fuck, Bill!?"

"John, consider it part of the investigation. It's totally within our authority. Consider it cheating fair."

"Holy shit!" John exclaimed. "I can't believe what I'm hearing."

"What, what are you talking about?"

"The last time I heard that expression was twenty-five years ago. Danbury said it when he persuaded me to lie to Gio about a contract hit on his life."

"What! What are you talking about?"

John was silent. He had carried this secret with him for twenty-five years and didn't mean for it to come out. He guessed it was a Freudian slip, whatever that really means. But it was out, subconscious or not, and if Bill was going to work with Gio on this case, it was just as well that he knows.

"We definitely expected a contract to be put out on Gio after he announced the existence of the family and his position as a capo at his sentencing. We knew he could help us with the bosses and had some intelligence that could also help us with Whitey Bulger's source at the Boston Bureau. Danbury convinced me that we should tell Gio we had evidence about a contract on his life and were well into the investigation. He had something on the warden at Big Sandy, because he just went along with it and authorized Gio's placement in the SHU for his protection."

Bill was listening intently with a straight look on his face.

"We found out that there was no contract. Gio's dad was legendary both here and in Sicily, which made Gio untouchable. Besides, he never named anyone, and the word got out that he wasn't talking to the Government. Where did you hear that line of bullshit, cheating fair?"

"I don't know, John. Somewhere. It was a stupid thing to say. But you didn't violate his constitutional rights. Law enforcement has been lying to suspects since the dawn of time. It's old law. It's been litigated."

"I don't give a shit about that, counselor. He was placed in the SHU because of it! I'm not going old law on Gio again. I'm the lead agent in this case, and the only way we're placing a bug under the table is if he agrees to it, and if he receives a written cooperation agreement, rather than us just bringing him back to court on a Rule 35."

Bill paused and thought about what he had just heard. He knew that a cooperation agreement with Gio would place the Government on more solid ground. They still had a strong case without Gio, but if he could help them get evidence through the Giattinos, it would be a quick guilty verdict.

"John, you're right. We'll do it your way."

"Thank you, Bill. I'm glad to hear that."

"It's all on you to get Gio on board."

"As it should be."

"Okay, Agent Taurino. I'll see you on Sunday for the big show, and you'll go pay Gio a visit the next day."

"Sounds good, Bill. I'll see you then."

Chapter 16

Mayor Danbury hadn't slept well since he separated from his wife and children. But his insomnia started long before that, as the stress of his circumstances began to grow. The trazadone wasn't helping him sleep, but a little cocaine was helping him get through his days. His comptroller had a supplier.

His life had become multi-layered, and he was having problems connecting all the dots and maintaining a clear separation between the people who knew the truth and those who did not. Lately, he was mindful of the only line of Shakespeare he remembered from college, "Oh what a tangled web we weave/When first we practice to deceive."

It started out small and simple: a promise with a handshake and nod of the head, campaign contributions, a new chimney, landscaping, in exchange for some unnamed future benefit—unnamed but eventually understood by way of implication and innuendo, a blind eye, conscious avoidance and so on and so forth. It started with the hazmat contractors, and Paul knew he needed help . . . allegiances. He had to build a team of loyal inspectors, supervisors, department heads. This wasn't hard because he had placed all his people in the right spots. He knew the intricacies of the scams; in fact, he had become an expert from his years on the White-Collar Crime Task Force. But when the big sharks started to smell blood— the Giattinos, to be specific—things became more complicated.

Paul was also an expert on money laundering, but his dealings with the brothers took his genius to a new height. Hiding half-a-million dollars was no small feat. He had saved copies of his old notes from when he prosecuted Ron Dumbkowski. That guy was good. He had created several shell corporations, along with fictitious executives, and kept it all in the States; no Swiss bank accounts or accounts on the Cayman Islands were needed. Ron's problem was, of course, a loss of control. Somebody caught in a bind with the Feds was always willing to help themselves, to whatever extent necessary, including wearing a wire.

Paul was empowered. The more he achieved, the easier it got. And it was never enough. It took up all his time, and Susan had had enough. He was either in the office or on the road, mostly in New York City dining and wining with Trump. But Susan was right. Even when he was home it was like they were separated. So, they might as well be separated for real.

When he first heard the loud bangs at the front door, he looked at the clock on the nightstand and saw that it was 5:30 am.

The banging continued at an even pace as he reached across the night table and opened the locked box that contained his Glock. It took a couple of seconds because his hand was shaking. The box opened, and the banging continued as Paul grabbed his pistol and slammed a loaded magazine into the handle.

He rushed toward the bedroom window, looked outside at the front and left side of the property, and saw the familiar blue windbreakers with FBI and IRS printed on the back. He walked back to the nightstand, placed his gun back in the lockbox, grabbed his stash from the dresser drawer and flushed it down the toilet as he heard a megaphoned voice: "Mr. Mayor, we have a warrant for your arrest and search and seizure warrants for your house. Please open the front door so we don't have to break it down."

Paul's mind was split between shock and resignation as he raced down the stairwell in his flannel pajamas. For months he had felt like he was driving his car on empty for miles, just waiting to run out of gas before he could get to a station.

The banging continued. "Mr. Mayor, this is your last warning!"

"I'm coming!" Paul shouted, as he tripped and almost took a nosedive down the final dozen steps. He could see the dark, distorted silhouettes of several agents through the stained glass of the double-wide front door.

After he opened the door, he was immediately surrounded by agents in their government- issued windbreakers. They all looked quite bulky, including the female agents, and Paul assumed they were wearing bulletproof vests. He was immediately addressed by a young female agent he didn't recognize.

"Paul Danbury, I'm Special Agent Sally Flowers, FBI. We have a warrant for your arrest on several charges, including racketeering, and a search and seizure warrant for your residence and office."

Paul was numb. He was looking at the young agent as she spoke.

"You have the right to remain silent."

She was short, about five feet tall.

"Anything you say can and will be used against you in a court of law."

He could see her short blond hair from under her FBI baseball cap.

"You have the right to be represented by an attorney."

She had a lovely face sprinkled with reddish-brown freckles.

"If you cannot afford an attorney, one will be appointed for you."

Paul was focused on Agent Flowers. He was aware of movement, the two dark shadows standing on either side of him. He could feel them breathing and could feel the movement of others throughout the house. But he was focused on Agent Flowers with a sort of tunnel vision. There was a kind of aura around her.

"Do you understand these rights that I've explained to you?"

Paul started to nod.

"You have to answer me, Mr. Mayor."

Paul heard himself say, "Yes, I understand," while pictures of his life began to flash through his mind. He didn't know if he was losing it, or if the sleepless nights and endless days had caught up to him. One of the two agents standing next to Paul said, "Mr.

Danbury, we're going to search you now," while Paul noticed the other agent click open a pair of handcuffs.

"Do you have any weapons on you, any needles or sharp objects on your person or in your pockets."

"No," Paul answered, hoping to wake up from his nightmare. The agent with the handcuffs stepped behind Paul.

"Please spread your legs apart and place your hands on top of your head."

Paul complied, and while being patted down, his attention returned to Agent Flowers, who was still standing in front of him. "Please place your hands behind your back," a voice spoke from behind him.

"Mr. Mayor, do you have any weapons in the house?" Agent Flowers asked.

"My Glock is in the lockbox on my night table next to the bed," Paul said, as he felt the cuffs secured around his wrist and heard the familiar sound of the grinding metal as they were locked in place.

"Is there anyone else home?" Agent Flowers asked.

"No. My wife and I separated, and she and the children are at her mother's place in Mount Pleasant."

"We know that, Mr. Mayor," replied Agent Flowers. "We waited until they moved out before coming, out of consideration for your family."

"Thank you," Paul said, as he realized he was never waking up from his new reality, which was dominated by his pounding brain and beating heart.

"I have here the two warrants I mentioned. You can read them, or they can be read to you while we search the house, but as you can see, we've already started searching your residence, and agents are presently searching your office at City Hall."

Paul looked around and saw a storm of activity, with at least a dozen agents and boxes already being carried out of the house.

"Yeah. We had to bring a big crew today. I knew the houses were big in Blackstone, but 10,000 square feet of three stories and a finished basement is a lot of space to cover," Agent Flowers said.

"I know the warrants are tight," Paul said. "Agent Taurino is a perfectionist." Paul knew Taurino had been a supervisor for years, and he knew in his gut that John was the lead agent on the case.

"As you know, you can stay while we execute the warrants if you'd like," Agent Flower said. "But you can't interfere in any way, or you will be charged with obstruction," she added. "I would recommend that you go along with agents Armstrong and Murphy to the U.S. Marshals facility downtown where you can be processed and allowed a phone call. The quicker you do that, the faster you can appear before Magistrate Fitzpatrick, who was kind enough to open her court on a Sunday for initial appearances."

"I'll go for the ride," Paul said.

Paul was very familiar with the U.S. Marshals Facility on Exchange Terrace in Providence. It was right next door to the historic federal courthouse. He had met with dozens of federal defendants in both facilities during his time as a prosecutor. He was not familiar with the body cavity strip search he suffered through in the lockup but was grateful to have the handcuffs removed. His headache had increased to a rhythmic throbbing in concert with his beating heart, amplified by the aching hunger in his gut. He had already called his attorney, Avrum Moskowitz, who was on his way to the courthouse for the initial presentment. He was placed in a long conference room with several rows of chairs. Then the Government's hit parade began to arrive.

The hazmat contractors came in first. They had paid his building inspectors tens of thousands of dollars over the years of his administration to sign off on the EPA regulations and allow unlawful disposal at the city dump. He didn't even know their names. He delegated that responsibility to Ronaldo Perez, his director of the Planning and Building Department, and his trusted comptroller, Patrick McMurphy, to keep him informed on the contracts and corresponding numbers. Paul built trust by delegating responsibility and empowering his direct reports. His mantra was Leadership on Every Level, the heading used to describe his administration in an article in *The New Yorker*, titled, "The 50 Top Mayors of America," published during his second term.

Perez and McMurphy were both brought in, along with a few small-time builders and contractors who he assumed had paid to earn contracts or be granted permits. Paul counted a dozen men, including himself. There was a small bathroom at the end of the room, and two marshals stood guard at both ends.

Paul was looking at the clock on the wall and trying to process that it was now 7:00 a.m., when three people entered the room, two women and a man. The man appeared to be middle-aged. He had broad shoulders, a neatly trimmed goatee, which was slightly graying, and sort of looked like a Hispanic George Clooney. He wore a dark blue pinstripe suit, with an off-white shirt and a red, paisley tie. The women were younger, probably in their mid-30s. They were both dressed professionally, but Paul didn't notice them as much, except that one was White with auburn hair, and the other was Black and wore cornrows. They each had files in their hands, and the women stood behind the man who spoke briefly with the marshal at the door before addressing the room.

"Good morning, gentlemen. My name is Jesse Garcia, and I am a senior U.S. probation officer. With me are officers Kim Lofton and Rebecca Miller. We work for the Court, today specifically for Magistrate Barbara Fitzpatrick. We are assisting the judge this morning in determining whether you can be released on some type of bond. We do that by conducting a quick investigation into your background, family, and community ties, your financial condition, and then make a recommendation to the Court. You can have an attorney present if you wish, but that will delay our investigations. Are there any questions? Okay then, we'll be coming around to have you sign some release forms and do interviews."

Paul declined to be interviewed, but all the other defendants appeared to be engaging in the process. He saw that it was 8:30 a.m. when the probation officers left the room.

Thereafter, two more marshals entered carrying leather belts and additional sets of handcuffs. The belts were thick and had large metal rings attached to the front and back. They were all told to stand against the wall leading to the door. Paul had been the first to enter the room and sat in the front row of chairs, so he was closest to the door and at the head of the line. A marshal placed the belt around his waist, secured the handcuffs around his wrists, in the front this time, and secured the handcuffs to the front ring with a large metal clip connecting the chain. Everyone was cuffed in this fashion.

They were instructed to turn to the side, at which point, two marshals approached Paul with a very long chain that had been retrieved from a large duffel bag. The chain was secured to the ring at the front of the belt, using the same clip, then slipped through the ring at the back of the belt; these same steps were taken for each man, securing the chain gang. They were marched out of the meeting room, down a long hallway and into a large elevator, where they were instructed to circle around and stand with their faces to the walls. Four marshals stood in the middle of the elevator, facing the men. They descended to the basement, then moved through a brightly lit tunnel that connected the building to the basement of the courthouse. They walked down another long hallway, then rode another elevator, in the same fashion, to the first floor that held the Marshals' facility adjacent to Judge Fitzpatrick's courtroom.

The men were unshackled and put in three connected holding cells. They placed Paul, Perez, and McMurphy in different cells, but they could all see each other. Nobody spoke. Most simply stared at the ground. Paul tried to concentrate on his breathing, using a technique he read about in an article about mindfulness and self-care. He remembered the name of the author, Dr. Petua Scorsi, from Fairfield University in Connecticut, and remembered the photo of a very attractive middle-aged woman with short blond hair, a friendly smile, and green eyes.

Paul had a great memory. It had always been one of his greatest assets. He worked on it and used it to his advantage. He remembered how to do cleansing breaths: breathe deeply through the nostrils, filling the lungs and solar plexus, out through the mouth, followed by a mindful mantra. His problem was that his mantra was Giattino, Giattino. Paul kept waiting for the brothers to appear. They didn't.

The initial appearances began at 10:00 a.m. Around that same time, FBI agents were delivering the target letters to the Giattino brothers, while Agent Taurino was sitting down for his second visit with Gio at FDC Devens.

There were two long conference tables in Judge Fitzpatrick's courtroom, which was in the newly added Annex at the back of the old courthouse. The defendants and their attorneys sat at one table, the Government at the other, and the three probation officers sat in the jury box. Avrum Moskowitz had assured Paul that he had contacted the probation officer and submitted a solid bond package. Bill Chin sat at the Government's table, along with his supervisor, Felix Fernandez. Paul didn't know who the young Asian prosecutor was, but he had hired Fernandez when he was the U.S. Attorney. Fernandez had aged gracefully. He obviously didn't believe in For Men Only and had solid strips of gray hair circling his head above his ears, and a neatly trimmed, fully gray beard. Felix had also bulked up, particularly around his midsection.

Bill Chin began with, "Your Honor, the defendant, Paul Danbury, is charged in 16 counts, one count each of racketeering, extortion, racketeering conspiracy, and bribery; two counts of bribery conspiracy; eight counts of mail fraud, and two counts of filing a false tax return. These charges result from a six-year scheme he orchestrated to shake down city contractors for more than $500,000 in cash, meals, clothing, wine, and home renovations."

The Judge then turned her attention to the defendant's table.

"Attorney Moskowitz, how does your client plea?"

Moskowitz and Danbury stood up together.

"Thank you, your honor. On behalf of my client, we enter not guilty pleas to all charges."

"Not guilty pleas are entered," Judge Fitzpatrick said. "And now we turn to the matter of bond."

"Yes, your honor. A bond package has been submitted to Officer Garcia and reviewed by the Government, and both the probation officer and Attorney Chin find it acceptable. I believe you have our proposal and the probation officer's pretrial report before you."

"Thank you, Attorney Moskowitz. I have met with Officer Garcia and discussed your package and understand that the Government has no objections. Is that correct, Attorney Chin?"

Bill stood up to address the Court, "Yes, your honor," then sat down.

"Very well. Mr. Danbury, I am releasing you on a $500,000 surety bond with conditions that you report to the United States Probation Office and comply with the standard and any special conditions of bond as instructed by the probation officer. Do you understand, Mr. Danbury?"

Paul stood up, "Yes, your honor," then sat back down.

"Very well. Mr. Danbury, you must now meet with a probation officer and sign your conditions of bond before you leave the courthouse today. Their office is right down the hall from my courtroom."

Paul and Moskowitz stood up. "Yes, your honor. I have reviewed the conditions with my client, and we are going to the probation office right now."

"Ok. I'll hear the charges on the next defendant, Attorney Chin."

Chapter 17

GIO WAS ALREADY SITTING in the interview room when John arrived. He stood up to greet him and shake his hand.

"Hi, John. It's a blessing to see you again."

"Gio, it's good to see you as well."

As they sat down, John again felt a sense of strength and peace within Gio. It was remarkable to him that this man could be so content after being locked up for almost 25 years.

"Gio, I have a lot to share with you today."

"I know you do. I had a dream about you last night. God gives me dreams sometimes."

"What was the dream?"

John was eager to know. He had contacted Greta Jones under the auspices of his investigation, and she had told him about Gio's dreams, his paintings, and the amazing things she had seen.

"I saw you sitting in a crowded courtroom. All the other people were a blur to me, but I saw you sitting in a chair, and I heard the words, 'You can rest now,' three times I heard it, 'you can rest now, you can rest now.'"

John didn't know what to say. He was distracted by the rush of adrenaline he felt. He took a moment and had to refocus.

"Gio, we arrested Danbury this morning along with eleven others, and we need your help."

John didn't know exactly how he would start this conversation, but he felt a sense of urgency and a need to be honest with this man.

"How can I help you, John?"

John felt strangely comfortable and at ease.

"Gio, your friends are in deep. Rory and Vinny weren't arrested but received target letters from the FBI. We know you're close with Vinny."

"I love him like a brother."

"I believe that. Look, we know the Giattinos have 'paid tribute' for as long as they've been around. It's the cost of doing business. But otherwise, they've been upstanding citizens, good Catholics with charitable hearts."

"They are both good men, and Vinny has come a long way in the past few years. He has grown in his faith."

"We see evidence of that. That's why we decided to send them a target letter in hopes that they decide to accept our offer to help us in this case, and in doing so, help themselves."

"That's very generous of the Government," Gio said with a hint of sarcasm in his voice that John immediately picked up on.

"Gio, look. I know how you feel about the way we treated you and wouldn't blame you if you told us to go fuck ourselves."

John suddenly felt awkward about dropping the F-bomb.

"Excuse me. I'm sorry about the language."

"That's okay, John. You don't have to apologize to me. Matthew 7:1 says, 'Judge not lest ye be judged.' It's taken me a while to get this. But I'm no one to judge another. Only God can judge. The Bible says that he knows the number of every hair on our heads. I believe he also hears every word we speak. I think that's the Holy Spirit making you uncomfortable."

Somehow, in a clear yet confusing way, John knew he would never use the F-word again and feel the same way about it. He felt like he was losing control of this interview and attempted to reel it back in.

"Gio, we—I mean, I—I mean we, the Government . . . Gio, I'm asking for your help. I know you're going to be seeing Vinny. He's been visiting you almost weekly since you got to Devens. Again, he and his brother are in deep and poured a lot of money into Danbury's pockets. We're not sure how much. Danbury evolved into some kind of genius money launderer, but your friends are looking at several years in prison based upon what we've put together so far."

The two men sat still for a couple of minutes without speaking.

"Gio. I think I've figured out a way to help you and make up for what I did to you all those years ago."

"When I told you I have forgiven you and Danbury, I was speaking the truth."

"I know that—"

"Please let me finish. I knew this day would come. Something you should know is that Vinny has accepted Christ and confessed his sins to me as God's word instructs. I have prayed for justice, but I have wrestled in the flesh, John. I had anger toward you and hatred toward Danbury, but the Bible explains everything in life that is conceivable to man. And God teaches and instructs on how to respond in any situation. Ephesians 6 says . . ."

Gio paused to examine John's heart.

"Do you want me to go on?"

"Yes. Please do."

"Ephesians 6:12, 13 says 'For our struggle is not against flesh and blood, but against the rulers, against the authorities, against the powers of this dark world and against the spiritual forces of evil in the heavenly realms.' Do you understand John?"

"I think I'm beginning to."

"It's spiritual warfare! The Lord tells us to put on the full armor of God, so that when the day of evil comes, you may be able to stand your ground, and after you have done everything, to stand."

Gio became emotional. Tears began to well up in his eyes, and his voice became shaky.

"I have tried to do everything to stand as a righteous man before God, a convicted murderer who has been forgiven."

"I'm not sure I understand. Everything you've done during your time, not just your prison record, but the things you've done, are amazing . . . I don't know Gio . . . I talked to Greta Jones . . . and the things she told me . . . I don't know . . ."

"John, I have been weak. Despite the years that I've been serving the Lord and all He has given me, I realized that I still held hatred in my heart for Danbury and believed that the only way I could avoid the sin of revenge was to stay out of it, completely out of it!"

"I think I'm starting to get it. No worries. We've got a solid case, and hopefully your friends will see the light."

"John . . . I'm not finished."

"Oh shit, I mean, damn, I mean, I'm sorry. Please go on."

"I've been praying about this, in faith. And God has answered my prayers," Gio said with a tone of peace and confidence in his voice. "God placed Matthew 5:44 on my heart, '. . . love your enemies and pray for those who persecute you.' Regardless of what's in your heart, John, what guilt or remorse you still carry, you are under the authority of God's ordinance, you are the lead agent on this case and come here in furtherance of a righteous investigation. However, I am not compelled to cooperate through obedience to Christ. God can deal with my unforgiveness and your guilt in his own way."

John was beginning to see through some sort of a cloud or fog in his mind that was starting to clear, and from a professional and practical sense in terms of his investigation.

"Okay," he said awkwardly, feeling foolish. And he continued to feel like he was screwing up when he added, "I don't know what to say."

Gio held up his hand.

"Stop. I don't want, or need, any contract with the Government."

"Okay."

John couldn't believe he said 'okay' again and kept stumbling through to the end.

"So Gio, I expect you'll receive a visit from Vinny soon."

"He's on my heart. He's my brother in Christ. I'm calling him this afternoon to find out when he can come."

"Okay," John said for the third time. He had simply stopped trying to act cool and just needed to get to the finish line.

"John, you are the lead agent. This is your investigation, and I've already heard from God on the matter."

"Okay then. I guess that's it."

Both men stood up.

"Gio, I am not sure I should say anything else at this time."

"Okay," Gio said in a humorous tone of voice.

"Thank you," John said and offered his hand.

Gio took John's hand, pulled him close and hugged him with intensity, while John awkwardly hugged him back. As he was about to exit the visiting room, Gio called out to him.

"John, I just have two more things to say to you before you leave. First, I love you, but more importantly, Jesus loves you."

"Okay," John said as he felt a big smile break out across his face.

Chapter 18

THINGS MOVED RAPIDLY AFTER John's visit with Gio.

The Giattinos came in and were fully forthright after signing cooperation agreements.

The trial took place before the Honorable Francis Black, who had taken senior status after 30 years on the bench. It was over in a week. Paul Danbury was permitted to represent himself and filed a few frivolous motions to exclude evidence. In his opening statement, he told the jury that he was not required to testify, cross-examine the Government's witnesses, or put on any witnesses of his own, and that it could not be held against him. The Government had to meet its burden of proof, and he believed the jury would find that they could not meet that burden. The Government's star witnesses of course were the Giattinos, followed by Ronaldo Perez, Patrick McMurphy, and a couple of hazmat and construction contractors. They all had cooperation agreements.

On March 19, 2015, Danbury was convicted of all 16 federal counts. He faced a possible sentence of up to 126 years, $500,000 in restitution, and $4 million in fines. Federal prosecutors asked for a sentence of ten years and one month, while Danbury asked for a sentence of no more than three years and ten months. Testimonials seeking leniency were filed with the court on his behalf, including one from Cardinal Edward M. Egan of New York.

On July 1, 2015, Senior U.S. District Judge Black sentenced Danbury to nine years in prison and a combined $750,000 in fines and restitution. During the sentencing hearing, Judge Black said that Danbury's crimes were the "stuff that cynicism is made of" and determined by clear and convincing evidence that Danbury had "lied to the jury during his closing argument when he denied any knowledge of fee-splitting deals and other incriminating evidence."

Six weeks later it was God's providence that Paul and Gio meet again.

Gio's appellate attorney had filed a motion for a special hearing, before Judge Nunez, to consider a reduced sentence based on Gio's extraordinary accomplishments during his term of imprisonment. The Judge was moved and wanted to see it happen. With the assistance of Magistrate Fitzpatrick, he had convinced the Government that it would be a worthwhile pursuit. He was now the chief judge, a powerful man, and the Government was wise to see the light of his reasoning. On that same day, Danbury was surrendering to the marshals to begin serving his sentence.

Gio was sitting alone in one of the holding cells when Paul was placed in the cell next to him. They were alone, as there was nothing else on the docket that day. As usual, Paul started the conversation.

"Mr. Bruno. It's funny how things work out, isn't it?"

"God does have a sense of humor."

"I'll say. That he does. That he does. We have to be able to laugh at ourselves or we'll go crazy. I heard about your conversion in prison. I'm so happy for you. You know I got saved at a Louis Palau conference last year."

"Amen, Counselor. I'm happy for you. Do you have a favorite verse that speaks to you?"

"Well of course. John 3:16, 'For God so loved the world that he gave up his only son so that whosoever believeth in him shall not perish but have everlasting life."

"Amen. Do you know Matthew 5:44?"

"No. I can't say that I do."

". . . love your enemies and pray for those who persecute you. . . ."

Gio was released that day after serving nearly 26 years and was placed on five years of supervised release. He met with Officer Garcia after the hearing to review the conditions of his supervision. Garcia had completed an updated presentence report for the court during which Gio learned that Jesse was a Christian brother.

Two years later, Gio was excited about seeing Jesse to tell him about his new change of employment. He had been working as a food server at Camille's since his release. The owner believed in second chances but also figured having a reformed mobster on staff would be good for business. He was right.

Gio had been distracted all day by scripture he didn't know. Philippians 2:14 had popped into his head that morning as he rode his bicycle to work, and he couldn't get it out of his mind. He had forgotten to bring his pocket Bible and didn't have one of those fancy iPhones with all the apps. He knew that Jesse loved the Word and planned on asking him about the verse.

When Jesse brought him into the office, Gio could see that he wasn't himself. He seemed angry and distant and was just going through the motions. Jesse was at his computer entering notes and wasn't even looking at him.

"Gio. What's the new job and the address? I'll have to check it out."

"Sure. Of course. I've got all the information here, and I'm so excited to share it with you. God is all over it, but I wanted to ask you a question first."

"Yeah. What's that?"

"Do you know Philippians 2:14?"

Jesse stopped what he was doing and turned to face Gio. "Oh—my—Lord. Thank you, Jesus."

"What? What is it? Do you know the verse?"

"Oh yeah. I know it but forgot it. God wrote it on my heart years ago."

"What is it? What does it say?"

"Gio, I've had a terrible week. I've been arguing with my supervisor about some cases on which we disagree, people have been coming to me for answers because they're too lazy to learn, and I've been complaining to my poor wife, who is kind enough to let me vent. Philippians 2:14 says, 'Do everything without arguing and complaining so that you may be blameless and pure children of God, without fault, in this crooked and depraved generation in which you will shine like stars in the universe. Thank you, Jesus, for bringing me back home.'"

"Amen," Gio said.

"Now tell me about that job of yours."

The following Monday, Gio was praying in the Spirit as he walked into his first day on the job as an art therapy counselor at Victory Outreach, a faith-based residential drug rehab in Cranston.

He paused before the front entrance to take a few cleansing breaths, and his mind became flooded with thoughts and emotions. He thought about his mama, his ex-wife, and Gio, Jr., about Carmine and his family, about the SHU, and Alex, about Taurino, Danbury, and Greta, and Christ. He could see Greta in front of her class. He was nearly overcome with love and gratitude. Her reference letter was invaluable in getting the job, along with all the courses he had completed. The director was also a recovering addict ex-convict.

Gio gathered himself, entered the building, walked into his classroom, stood before his students, and began.

"Art is a gift from God, through which he can create a path to healing."

The End